Young Writers

what's the story?

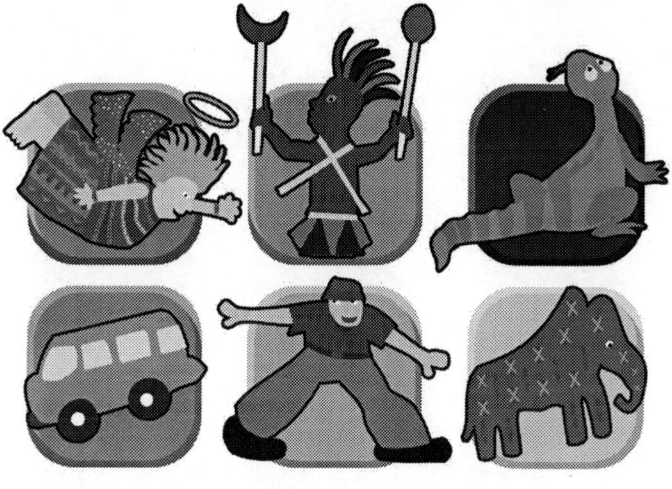

London Vol II

Edited by Steve Twelvetree

First published in Great Britain in 2003 by
YOUNG WRITERS
Remus House,
Coltsfoot Drive,
Peterborough, PE2 9JX
Telephone (01733) 890066

SB ISBN 1 84460 301 6

FOREWORD

This year, Young Writers proudly presents a showcase of the best short stories and creative writing from today's up-and-coming writers.

We set the challenge of writing for one of our four themes - 'General Short Stories', 'Ghost Stories', 'Tales With A Twist' and 'A Day In The Life Of . . .'. The effort and imagination expressed by each individual writer was more than impressive and made selecting entries an enjoyable, yet demanding, task.

What's The Story? London Vol II is a collection that we feel you are sure to enjoy - featuring the very best young authors of the future. Their hard work and enthusiasm clearly shines within these pages, highlighting the achievement each story represents.

We hope you are as pleased with the final selection as we are and that you will continue to enjoy this special collection for many years to come.

CONTENTS

The Stories

THE STRANGE LAND

Tom was reading a book. He opened the next page. The book was pulling Tom inside. He was in an enormous jungle. The trees were blue, yellow and red. On the trees were fish with legs. As well, the sky was all different colours.

Suddenly he saw a strange dragon. The thing had long, dotted horns. As well, instead of wings it had arms and hands and claws like a dragon's. Tom felt amazed. *Will this dragon attack me?* thought Tom.

Suddenly the dragon spoke. James was amazed.
'Hello I'm Spike,' explained the dragon.
'I need your help,' mumbled Spike.
'Why?' said Tom.
'Because my little brother was kidnapped in a cave,' said Spike, 'by the evil ogre,' explained Spike.
'I will help you,' said Tom.

So Tom and Spike set off.
They walked day and night. At last they saw a gigantic cave.
'Let's go,' whispered Spike. They walked silently inside. It was dark and slimy. There were bats on the black, dark, gloomy walls.
'I'm terrified,' shouted Tom.

Suddenly they saw a massive ogre. Luckily Tom saw a fat stick. So he grabbed the stick and bashed it on the ogre. The ogre fell down. *Bash!* Tom and Spike saw a gold key in the ogre's hand. So they opened the cage and Spike's brother came out and they ran away.
'But I need to get home,' said Tom.
'You have to get out of the book,' explained Spike.
'But how?' asked Tom.
'There's no time. We have to get you home,' said Spike.
So they walked day and night. At last they were there.
'Go through that book,' explained Spike.
'OK,' said Tom. 'Bye-bye.'

'I'm home,' said Tom. 'Yippee!'

Reade Mulvany (8)

1

THE CHINA DOLL

One day when Christy and Joanne were walking home from school they saw a china doll inside of a shop window. When they bought it they went home, chucked their bags on the floor and went down to dinner.

Later, when they went upstairs they went to bed and placed the china doll on the bedside unit. In the middle of the night Christy went downstairs to get a glass of milk, but when she came back up she saw Joanne on the floor with blood pouring from her head.

As Christy turned around to run, the china doll was blocking her way! With one mighty swing from his knife he killed her and laid her down next to Joanne. Then he cackled . . .

100 years later

One day two buyers came into the house and saw the same china doll upon the floor.
The china doll suddenly said, 'Someone's gonna die today!' and then he cackled.

Jack Howard (10)
All Saints CE Primary School

THE LITTLE BIG SURPRISE

One summer's day, in the countryside where the birds sang and the bees flew, a pretty young girl by the name of Maria decided to visit the woods, as she had never been there before. Maria was adventurous and she would never give up in anything she did. Maria couldn't wait as she loved nature and animals. First of all Maria decided to climb the tallest tree right to the top.

Suddenly, in the distance, Maria could see a golden glow. She decided to investigate straight away. As she got closer, the glow became brighter and when Maria finally reached the golden glow she so much desired to see, she paused for a while and stared. It was hard to tell what the shape was. It looked like an egg but there were no birds' nests around so Maria decided to take the egg to look after.

Maria made a nest for the egg out of soft feathers and four comfy pillows to keep the egg glowing. Maria kept the egg close to her at night and she wrapped it in four thin handkerchiefs with a ribbon to hold it together, in the daytime when she went to school. Maria didn't tell anyone about the egg because it was hers and only hers.

It had been about two weeks since she had found her egg. It was about seven o'clock in the evening. Maria was upstairs caring for her golden egg. Maria could see small cracks in her egg. It was hatching! What could be inside the golden egg? Maria saw a small wing and soon a fairy was revealed! The fairy thanked Maria for looking after her and gave her a small wand.

'Wave this wand and say, olay, olay Minnie me land! The words will take you to fairyland and you can visit whenever you like!' said the small fairy. The fairy left Maria and flew to her home. How happy Maria was!

Natasha Luthra (10)
All Saints CE Primary School

THE RED RUBY

It all happened in a little cottage called Ilram. There were many trees and every morning, the birds would fill the air with the most beautiful sound. There were three poor children who were abandoned by their cruel parents; Lucy, Flora and Daniel. Flora was the oldest and was the most beautiful of them all. She was funny and always had much good luck. Then came Lucy who was very industrious but she could be very greedy at times. Last came Daniel, who always started off the fight but good at figuring out solutions.

One sunny day they decided to go on the cliff to admire the wonderful sunset. However, Daniel disobeyed and stamped out of the door because he hated wasting time. Luckily, Lucy managed to catch him but Daniel kicked her and she fell off the cliff pulling Daniel and Flora with her.

Somehow, when they woke up they felt something soft and fluffy. They opened wide their eyes when they saw where they were. There were flowers with colourful petals and soft grass. When you felt it, it gave you a great feeling inside. In front of them was a big yellow door written: *Beware, beware, the dragon's lair, in you go if you dare.* The children were very fond of adventures and with one small hand, they turned the doorknob quietly.

It was very calm inside with two old doors on both sides. They decided to go in the right door. To their surprise, the room was filled with many valuable things. Suddenly, there was a growl and behind them was a red dragon gazing anxiously at them. They ran out of the door to the left with the dragon behind them.

Lucy stopped at one corner and with the tip of her finger, she accidentally touched a red button. A brown door opened and they hurried into the door and closed it within one second. There, they came out and to their astonishment they were once again back home.

Meanwhile, the dragon was confused where they had gone. The children went back to the cottage and realised that they had taken a big red ruby and they decided to keep it and would remember what had happened. They'll never forget . . . whatever happens!

Szi Kay Leung (10)
All Saints CE Primary School

WITCHES, WITCHES

'Come on Son, we need to go to the Splodgeville Woods,' shouted Dad.
'Coming!' he answered.
'Let's go and pick up your friends Alex, Michael, Sunil and Yashar.'

'Here we are at Splodgeville Woods where the famous witch stories are told.'
'Did . . . did you say witch?' asked Michael in a frightened voice.
'Yeah, I did say witch,' said Dad.
'You mean you're scared of witches Michael?' said Yashar.
'Can we just light the fire please!' said Michael.

'Once upon a time there lived a boy who was called Jason. Jason was a strong and brave boy with light brown hair and brown eyes. Jason believed in witches and he was loaded with protection to kill witches and this is when he went face to face with what he believed in.

Jason couldn't believe his eyes! He was face to face with a witch. All Jason did was panic. Even though he was a strong and brave boy he remembered garlic kills witches! So he ran to the local shops, bought some garlic and rushed back to the pack. 'There you go,' said Jason. He threw the garlic at the witch. The witch screamed! Then the witch disappeared and Jason hurried home.'
'So witches do exist!' said Yashar.
'No they don't!' exclaimed Michael.

Adam Tzimas (10)
All Saints CE Primary School

A Day In The Life Of Ruby The Dog

I wouldn't have been the dog that I am now if it wasn't for that special day which changed my life completely.

Well I was the boring, old, authentic-faced, dribbly dog, who didn't get any respect from anyone for whatever I did until . . .

One day Simon called me, 'Ruby!' He was calling my name from upstairs. We had a little cottage in the countryside, with a big plant called Broom just coming over our front door. Inside the house it was time for dinner. I was so hungry that I ran my fastest to my bowl but when I got there there was an abrupt stop. *Splat!* Right in my bowl, some leftover, sloppy, disgusting food mixed in soup. Suddenly I didn't feel very hungry. They used to treat me terribly, like I didn't exist.

Late at night when everyone was asleep, I looked into the night's sparkly sky, when there was a slight squeak at the door. I went to see what it was, but when I did my eyes grew wider and wider for there was a burglar in the house! I started to bark continuously, then Simon and his parents woke up. The burglar was holding Simon's parents' precious ring! I just couldn't let him go so I bit his leg and the police soon caught up with him.

I was rewarded with a golden medal and a sloppy kiss and that's how I became special.

Sotiria Kyriakou (10)
All Saints CE Primary School

HAUNTED HOUSE

Once upon a time in England there were two boys called Ben and Bill. They asked their grandad if they could go up the High Road for a walk and Grandad said, 'OK.'
They said, 'Thank you Grandad,' and then they walked out of the front door.

They walked up the High Road and then they saw an old house with the door open. They went inside and there was glass everywhere. They went upstairs - there was glass upstairs too. Upstairs the lights were off.

Suddenly they saw a ghost, *'Raa!'*
They screamed and couldn't see anything. The ghost was right behind them so they turned the light on and then somehow the ghost just disappeared. Ben said, 'Ghosts mustn't like light.' And they ran home as fast as they could.

Daryl Ruskin (10)
All Saints CE Primary School

THE MYSTIC DOLL'S HOUSE

I woke up but it was still 1.03am. Something was drawing me to my sister's doll's house. You see, it's shaped like our house and the dolls are like our family, but when I looked closer there was another person with a dagger in his hand in my brother Pete's room. Then there was a spine-cracking scream and the sound of smashing glass. I realised my brother had been murdered. I ran to my mum's room and shouted, 'Peter has been murdered!'

On the 20th of June (two weeks later) on BBC2 news, a report announced that Peter's murderer had been caught and sentenced to 30 years in jail, but the following week he broke out.

The next night I woke up again. It was 1.03am and this time I was drawn to the wardrobe. I opened it - he was there! I ran into the hall and into a closet. He saw me and threw his dagger. It missed. I ran to my sister's doll's house.

I knew a few tricks now - one is wherever the doll or object is, that's where the thing is, so I decided to move the murderer off my brother. But where to? I know, the roof. I quickly moved the figure onto the roof and called the police.

Next morning I won a bravery medal and the murderer won a lifetime in jail.

Adem Ikibiroglu (11)
All Saints CE Primary School

SLEEPOVER HELL

'Lewis, I'll go and get the sweets for our midnight feast while you load the PlayStation,' Richard shouted. It was a perfect night for a midnight feast because Richard's family were away. Just then the phone started to ring. I thought it was really strange for someone to be ringing at that time of night, but then I thought it was probably his mum.

'Hello Mum, yeah, I'm fine, just going to bed now, bye,' I could hear Richard saying. Suddenly I heard Richard shouting, 'Lewis, Lewis, help.' Then I heard a bang and then everything went silent. I knew something was wrong so I made my way downstairs. That's when I saw Richard was dead. He was lying on the floor with a huge puddle of blood around him and a gun was on the table. I was shaking but I went to the phone - the phone line was dead, just like Richard.

I waited for about a minute then I decided to ring the police. When I picked up the phone I could hear someone speaking. They were saying to me, 'In a couple of minutes you will be dead as well. Look in the fridge and you'll see why.' Without thinking twice I had a look in the fridge. Inside there was a huge snake with sharp, black teeth. Without thinking again I picked the gun up from the table. I pulled the trigger and the snake let out a hiss. I decided to run in case the snake was still alive. I looked back, the snake had regained health and was coming after me. I jumped out of the window and landed with a few cuts and bruises.

Lucky for me a police car came around the corner and I told them everything.

Lewis Ford (11)
All Saints CE Primary School

THE DARE

I was regretting saying yes to Melody's dare. I had to play knock-down-ginger on Mrs Slice's door. She was an old lady and a bit gone in the head.

'Well go on then!' Melody said, with her hands on her hips. There I was standing there with my finger, half a centimetre away from the doorbell. I could feel my sweat running down my neck onto my back, my hand was shaking hard, so were my legs.

Ding-dong. The bell rang. Melody ran down the road leaving me standing there shaking even harder. All over me felt so hot, like a boiling kettle. The door slowly creaked open and there she was, Mrs Slice, standing there with a long silver knife in her hand ready to chop me up into bits.
'Argh!' I screamed. I was so scared I kicked the 69-year-old lady over. She fell to the floor, not moving. She was dead.

I ran as fast as I could, but at the end of the road were two coppers. I tried to act normal, but I gave in and had to tell them everything.

They took me to the police station. I went in a room and they asked me questions. I was in a cell.

Five minutes later I saw Melody. She came in my cell too. We looked at each other in shame. My life was finished, I would never be the same person again.

Ellis Higgins (11)
All Saints CE Primary School

THE SLEEPOVER

On Friday the 13th I slept round my friend's house. Me and Tom had been playing on the PC and were about to complete the game when his mum came in and said, 'Thomas, Richard, go to sleep.' Then his mum shut the door and we got into bed.
'I'm not tired,' said Richard.

As I pulled the sheet over me I could hear a creak. Then something was coming out of the computer. I woke up Tom and said, 'Look!'
Tom jumped in fright, then we woke up his mum and she came to have a look and when she got there and said, 'There's nothing here boys.' Then she looked again and said, 'Run!'

Tom's mum woke his dad and then we all got in the car. We went to my house and they all slept over at mine.
My mum came in and said to us, 'Do you want to watch some TV to calm down?'
After we watched TV we went to bed.

Me and Tom got into our bed and played cards without my mum knowing. Then we tried to get to sleep but couldn't really. We heard our parents go to bed. Me and Tom finally got to sleep.

I woke up in the middle of the night, but who knows what could be in my house when there was a ghost in Tom's?

Richard Warner (11)
All Saints CE Primary School

CHASE OF MY LIFE

'Mum, I'm going to Joe's house,' I shouted as loudly as I possibly could.
'OK,' she replied in a loud voice.

I set off to Joe's house. As I got there I saw another boy my age running down the street. I wondered what had happened so I ran as speedily as I could. I saw Lisa (Joe's mum) standing outside the house.

'Red (that's me), Joe has been chased into the dark, gloomy woods,' she explained.
I ran down the street as quickly as I could. Then, as I was running, I caught a glimpse of a stockily-built person, but he was running towards me. Just then I saw Joe lying on the floor bleeding. I knew the person who was running towards me had shot Joe, so I jumped on top of him and got the gun. As soon as I got it I called the police.

They came as quickly as they could, but by the time they got to us the man had got away.

I was chasing him, followed by the police. When I got to him I realised he was too strong so I bundled him. Just then I remembered about Joe, so I ran back to him but when I reached him I noticed I was bleeding too, then I fainted. And now I'm in hospital . . .

Bilal Hussain (11)
All Saints CE Primary School

THE SPOT

Twelve midnight struck, Danny shivered, he wasn't cold, you wouldn't be on a summer night at all. No Danny wasn't cold just afraid, very, very afraid.

You see, Danny had just walked by a very strange spot, the spot was strange due to a hundred murders that have occurred there over a hundred years, and the bodies had all been found on that particular spot. The same had happened this year.

You see, people like Danny are superstitious, they believe what they hear and suggest conclusions but some people don't know how right they are.

Danny hurried on, first walking then jogging, then running violently. He knew there was something behind him, but what? Suddenly it began to rain. Danny slowed down and ran into a phone booth.

He began panting heavily. He could hear faint footsteps outside the booth. Suddenly a shadow appeared before Danny. The shadow chuckled an evil laugh, its red eyes glared with anger.
'What do you want?' Danny cried.
'Ha, ha, ha, *death!*'
And with that Danny met his doom and the shadow beheaded the poor boy and the next day something was rotting on the spot - the rotting thing was poor Danny's body.

Minil Patel (11)
All Saints CE Primary School

THE CHINA DOLL

It was early in the morning of Millie's birthday. She had just woken her mum and dad. They all went downstairs and next to the sofa were Millie's presents. She ripped open all of them. Millie got some great stuff but she was mostly looking forward to her auntie's present.

Suddenly the postman knocked on the door. She threw open the door and snatched the present then ran upstairs. Her parents had made her a birthday breakfast. She had opened her present and all it was, was a China doll. Millie just threw it on the floor.

At lunchtime Millie went back up to her bedroom and her China doll was sitting on the bed. Millie just stared at it.
Suddenly the China doll said, 'I'm going to get you.'
Millie ran downstairs. The only noise she made was, 'Argh!'

She was sitting on the sofa shaking when her mum and dad shouted, 'We're going to the shops, you stay here.'

When the door shut, the China doll was sitting next to her and said in a cute and evil voice, 'I'm going to get you.'
Millie ran outside the house. When her parents got back Millie went straight to bed with no sign of the China doll.

The next morning Millie woke up and went downstairs to find the China doll, but it was nowhere to be seen. Then Millie heard a bang in the kitchen cupboard. She opened the cupboard and 'Argh!'
The China doll had taken her. Millie was never seen again.

Georgia Gowland (10)
All Saints CE Primary School

THE HAUNTED HOUSE

In the middle of the night three boys and three girls were walking home from a pub. Their names were William, Adam, Nick, Georgia, Katie and Emma. They all were walking until they stopped and found themselves in front of a house.

It looked like a rich man's house. William knocked on the door - nothing happened. Emma knocked the door open and they went inside. Adam shouted if anyone was there - no reply. They went inside the house. Georgia wanted to go home.

The door closed shut. William got his handgun out. There was a creak and loads of arrows shot straight for them. Adam, Emma, Nick and Katie died. William and Georgia tried to get out but a vampire bit them and they turned into vampires.

They killed anyone who came past the haunted house. Nine people have died from coming into the house.

A man came along to look for William. He was the police. He opened the door and saw William and Georgia.

The policeman looked at William and Georgia and they captured them. He found out what they were. They were taken away and the haunted house was annihilated.

William and Georgia were safe for now, well they hoped . . .

William Maynard (10)
All Saints CE Primary School

16

CLOWNS

My mum booked a holiday for us. Great! Well almost, you see it was on Friday the 13th of August in an old house, and old houses are always haunted. Help!

Today was the day I was going on holiday. After a long day of travelling, we finally reached our destination. A 'hotel', yeah right!

My mum put the key in the door, turned the handle and the door creaked as she opened it. We walked in slowly. There were cobwebs everywhere, yuck. My mum took me upstairs to my room, but there weren't any cobwebs up there, only pictures of clowns everywhere. I looked at them in a freaked out way.

That night when my mum was in bed, I decided to look around the house. As I was going down the stairs I heard footsteps very faintly, but I ignored them. I went to the kitchen to get a drink but I trod in some liquid. I switched the light on and I saw a pile of blood - scary or what? I heard the footsteps again but louder. I turned round and there was a clown holding a knife. I screamed.

I ran past the clown, upstairs and locked myself in my room, but the clowns in my room started to move and chase me. I jumped out the window but another clown caught me.
'Argh, help!'

Charlotte Sykes (10)
All Saints CE Primary School

DISASTER STRIKES IN THE ISLE OF WIGHT

It was the third day of Year 5's school journey. They were all excited because they were to do caving as an activity. Phillip and Shaun raced downstairs to say good morning to Rachel, the prettiest girl in their class. The class was split into two groups P and Q. P's challenge was that they had Lazer Quest while Qs had to go-kart. Once they had finished those it was lunchtime.

'Go on Luke, keep going, beat her. Yes!' screamed Paul.
Luke had won the race because Rachel kept looking at her nails while she was driving.

It was lunchtime and after that it was time for the *caves!* As they approached the caves they could smell a disgusting smell of dirty water. Rachel didn't want to go in because she thought she would smell. They all started crawling through obstacles and over planks, then suddenly . . . *bang! Bang!* It was a gunshot - of all the people James had been shot.

Rachel started to cry because James was her boyfriend. Could this be the end of their trip?

That afternoon Year 5, Miss Hamilton, Miss Trapani and Mrs Milton left. Mrs Milton asked who had shot James, but no one answered. The prime suspects were Phillip, Shaun and Miss Hamilton.

Rachel found a tape on the ground. She played it to the class. It said, 'I have to kill him. I hate him.' It was Miss Hamilton's voice but she wasn't in the caves, so who had shot James?

James Gray (11)
All Saints CE Primary School

THE DOOR

I tossed and turned all night. The wind seemed to be screaming my name, and the trees waving their arms in protest. I crept out of bed and into the hall. The door creaked and then revealed an oak staircase. My feet chilled as soon as they hit the cold floor.

I heard a groan. I turned around and tried to figure out where the noise was coming from. I came to a door, then found a key on the table. I opened the door, shaking. Dust spurted out and guided me to a room. A giant man sat at a table, his hair was mangled, his skin looked stretched over his bones.

In the room was a table made out of stone, also used as a bed. The only glorious thing about the room was a clock.
'What do you want?' said a gruff voice.
'Who are you?' I said.
'I'll show you.'

Just then the clock sounded one o'clock. Colours whizzed and furniture flew, then a picture formed. We were now in a different room - grand and Victorian. A lady entered, she looked like she could freeze laughter. There was a well-heeled boy next to her. The lady turned and dragged the boy off. The colours whizzed and we were back.

'That boy was me, and this is my house!' said the man.
'You must be my grandad?'

Katie Guild   (10)
All Saints CE Primary School

THE MURDER IN THE DARK

Ben was at Scout parade in the church. There were high-heeled footsteps to be heard outside. Suddenly there was a snip - the lights went out. Instantly there was a flash of blinding light. On the floor the vicar was seen in a puddle of blood, dead.

The next day Ben was taken to a police station. He told the police exactly what had happened. A policeman called Badge was assigned to catch the murderer. Ben didn't find Badge helpful at all. All he did was stand staring with a note book. Ben had to think harder about what had happened. Suddenly it came to him - the snip he'd heard before the lights went out.

He ran to the church as fast as he could and found under a table were some clippers with a gun installed to them. There was also a tube that could have sucked out the air that the bang of the gun would travel through. Ben climbed under the table. There was the broken wire. Somehow an extra battery pack was attached, keeping the ends together. Ben noticed that there was electricity flowing out of the extra pack.

From under the table a scream told the police something was wrong. They followed the scream and found Ben lying dead next to, what the evidence had shown as, the murderer. Ben had caught the murderer under the table, but the electricity from the added battery pack had killed them both. Ben was considered a hero.

Scott Fisher (11)
All Saints CE Primary School

ESCAPE FROM AFRICA

I was shipped to Africa when I was little. My mum said goodbye and there I was all on my own in Africa.

I had been there a couple of months when I had to go to the market. Suddenly someone grabbed me. I screamed; she told me to be quiet.

We walked for ages until we stopped by an old, rusty van. I hadn't seen the lady till we got in the van. She was a young lady. She told me her name was Mary. She also told me that she was taking me home because the people looking after me were going to kill me. She started to drive away.

We stopped at a ship. Mary told me to get out quietly and stay close. Then she said we were going to sneak onto the ship. On the ship we hid around every corner so no one would see us. We finally found a place to stay, in the cellar behind some boxes.

We had been on the ship for about a week. Suddenly two men grabbed us and took us up deck. Mary mouthed something to me. The men held knives to our throats. Then Mary grabbed my hand and we jumped onto the lifeboat and sailed off.

We grew very close. We ended up going to America. I never saw my mum again, but Mary was good enough for me.

Bronia Burlinska (11)
All Saints CE Primary School

HORROR HAPPENING IN TOWN

It was Thursday 12th October, the day before Friday the 13th October when werewolves come out, witches make their potions and ghosts are in the air.

The door creaked, my brother was scared.
'It's only mum and dad coming back from shopping,' I said.
It felt weird, it was like they were under a spell. Now I knew tomorrow was going to be a bad day.

The worst day of my life had come. The radio said the schools were closed as there was a storm ahead. I was really freaked out. I knew they were coming - werewolves waiting in streets, witches' laughter, zombies waking by the sound of the storm.

It came to night-time, I couldn't sleep. I found out my mum and dad were under a spell - the zombie's spell.

I had to get out of the house before they made me a zombie. I ran outside, it was raining. I was very worried now. It was dark and cold. I had no coat and I was freezing. My family were already under a spell. I was walking, zombies were surrounding me. I ran into the nearest house, but I chose the wrong house. Stood there were three witches and ghosts. The spirit of me was gone forever and ever.

Until now . . .

Leigh Hagger (11)
All Saints CE Primary School

PERFECT MATCH

I woke up feeling better than ever. The sun was shining high in the sky. I got ready for college and then it happened, I was walking towards the bus stop when I saw a really good-looking boy waiting at the bus stop, his teeth were so shiny it hurt to look at them. I stood next to him and he said, 'Hi.' His voice was so soft and gentle. We sat next to each other on the bus, the journey went quickly and then I said, 'Well this is my stop, see you.' I got off and so did he. I got into college and the bell rang and we all rushed to get somewhere.

On the way I bumped into the lovely boy again. My books fell on the ground so we both bent down and looked into each other's eyes and he said, 'Hi again.' I told him that my name was Becky and he told me his was Charlie. Then we both started to pick up the books.

All day I couldn't stop thinking about him. Then it clicked with me, this could be my chance, *I'll ask him to go to the prom with me on Friday night.* I asked him and he said yes. I just couldn't believe my luck. I had finally met the perfect guy.

It was Friday. (*Yes*, I thought). Me and my friends got ready and I walked through the door and reached Charlie. He said, 'You look amazing.'
I replied, 'You don't look too bad yourself.' We laughed all night and it felt great.

Isabella Di Giuseppe (10)
All Saints CE Primary School

MR STONEY'S BIG ADVENTURE

One day I was walking down a beach in France. I saw something that caught my eye. It was a stone. Not just any old stone, it was a stone that was two thousand years old. It probably saw Sir Walter Rayleigh set off to explore the United States of America. So I picked up the stone and went back to London to my school. On the way I felt a tingle in my hand. I looked under my hand; the stone was growing legs. I was surprised.

The next day I took the stone to school. I was walking with my friends and I was walking with the stone. We were playing football. My friend said to the stone, 'Hello how are you doing today?'
'Fine,' the stone said.

The bell rang - time to start school. My teacher Miss Wooldrige said, 'Who is he then Hayden?'
'My friend the stone. We could call him Mr Stoney.'

We had English and maths. At lunchtime Stoney and I went for the seafood. I hated it because they didn't add the spices.

Then we had science and history. Mr Stoney was very good at those subjects; he even got a headteacher's award. Miss Wooldrige was very pleased.

'Thanks for a great day Hayden,' said Stoney.
'That's alright!' I replied.

Hayden Skervin (10)
Broadwater Primary School

THE MOTHER IN THE CHAMBER

'Dean come downstairs, it's dinnertime!' Mum shouted from the kitchen.
'OK Mum, I'm coming!' I bellowed from my bedroom. I came down when suddenly the doorbell rang. Mum opened it with a sigh. Astonishingly no one was there.

Anyway, we got on with dinner, we had chicken with roast beef. It was scrumptious. After dinner Mum was asking me about my birthday party. So we wrote the invitations and put them into the envelopes.

The next day I went and posted them. Everyone came to my birthday party and Mum opened the windows for fresh air. It was very strange, the last doorbell that Mum heard, she opened it and no one was there. Then it happened again. This time Mum got anxious and phoned the police. The police came and waited on the other side of the door to see who it was.

While we were all having dinner, I had a feeling that something bad was going to happen. I opened my presents. My favourite one was the Xbox.

The party was over and everyone was going home. Then suddenly I realised Mum wasn't there. I knew something was going to happen. I looked for her everywhere, even in the attic. I went outside, I was about to ask the police but they had gone too. I slammed the door and then I saw a note and this is what it read.

'Dear Dean,
Your mother has gone.
Forever!
I hate her. Her body will lie in the chamber.
From . . . '

Amnah Rehman (10)
Broadwater Primary School

THE MASK

Jack climbed down the ladder from his tree house because there was nothing to do there, he was bored. He called out, 'I'm going for a walk.' 'OK,' shouted his mother.

Jack started to walk down the road. *There is nothing to do in this town,* Jack thought. Jack and his mum had just moved to this town a week ago and it was already boring. As he was walking he saw an object lying in some dust. Jack walked over to it, it was rusty. He realised it was a mask. He tried it on but then suddenly he couldn't control himself at all.

Jack started banging himself into things but of course it wasn't him, it was the mask. But it wasn't just the mask, it was the spirit inside it. Jack went in front of a car and got hit by it, but he didn't even get hurt. He just carried on walking. He was going back to his house.

When Jack got home he went to his mother and started hitting things around her.
'What are you doing? Stop it!' she cried.
'*What!*' Jack bellowed.
'Stop it!' she yelled. 'Why are you wearing that mask on your face? Remove it!'
'No!' Jack cried.
'Well I will,' she shouted and pulled it off. 'What happened?'
'Huh?' Jack said.
She explained what happened. 'Could it be the mask?'
'Let's see,' Jack said. He picked it up and burnt it. She was right.

Camilla Dhunnoo (10)
Broadwater Primary School

THE ADVENTURE OF THE SECRET HOLE

While Simvit was eating his breakfast he heard a strange noise. It was coming from his back garden. It always sounded like a blurring noise. It was a scary noise with a clue. Simvit wanted to go to the back garden. So he went off. It was coming from the secret hole that Dad dug up. Inside was very mouldy, but Simvit didn't care. So he went inside. The door banged shut.

'Very dark,' murmured Simvit. It began to start raining. He could hear the raindrops spluttering on the top of the tunnel. 'Scary, scary, Mummy and Daddy,' he whispered softly. He was sitting under something comfortable, it was a feather, that didn't really help.

The next morning Simvit was awoken by a gush of water. He kept sliding around in circles, he tried holding on to something, but it was too thin. *Bang!* 'Arghh,' he wailed. Down he fell into a secret tunnel again. He landed on top of a frog called Froggie.
'Greetings, greetings I shall tell you the way out of here at once!'
'Okay, thank you,' replied Simvit.

So the frog was followed by Simvit, at last they came to the end of the tunnel. Locked! Froggie ran back and ran forward, bashed with his head to open the door. They both got out. *Boom!* A cloud of steaming hot smoke spread. The tunnel began to break. *Slap!* Simvit's dad slapped him. Simvit knew that the tunnel was his dad's. He got grounded for one month. *Bad!*

Anique Rehal (10)
Broadwater Primary School

RAISING THE DEAD

I was coming out of school when I saw Joey and Kasandra. They were looking like they were on cloud nine. I hadn't seen them so happy for a long time so I went over to ask them why they were so happy.

They replied, 'We're going to the graveyard.' And they asked me, 'Want to come tomorrow?'

Then I said the weirdest thing. 'Sure I'd love to.' I don't know why I said it but I did.

The next day I called Joey. (You might think it's a boy's name but that's another story.) When I called her she said, 'Be ready at midnight,' and that was the last thing she said before she hung up.

At midnight I snuck out of my window and went to the graveyard at 1am. No one was there so I was just about to leave, then I saw this freaky lady.

She came to me and said, 'You are to marry her to raise all the dead, evil ghosts.'

I saw a stick and threw it. I had a chance to run, so I did.

Craig Archer (10)
Broadwater Primary School

THE SLAYERS

In the heart of Collosus mountain village a big execution took place in a small prison. Frank Tester was being executed for creating a virus which would kill millions of innocent people.

During that event the antidote slipped out of the container and turned all the people into hideous beasts. Four guardians however survived. Their names were Avenger, he possessed an axe and an old rifle. The next survivor was called Gudge, he had a sword and a crossbow. Next was Derender, she possessed a katana and a magnum revolver. The last person was Martyr, she wasn't a guardian, she was a normal girl equipped with two pistols and two daggers.

These four fighters were determined to wipe out as many beasts and zombies as they could and save all the innocent people.

Throughout their quest they fought many battles and saved many civilians.

When they got onto the main road they saw a vampire who looked just like Frank Tester from all those years ago. But there was one difference, he was a vampire. The guardians were attacked by him. They fought back fiercely and freed the hostages that he kept. That was the end, well that's what they thought . . .

To be continued!

Emil Torrens-White (10)
Broadwater Primary School

MR STONEY'S BIG ADVENTURE

One day I was walking near a waterfall when a stone fell straight on my round head. I fell unconscious and when I woke up, I saw a spotty, greyish stone with white dots. It felt smooth as it had been smothered by the sparkling sea. It looked very unusual because it had two holes underneath. So I took it with me.

When I was on the bus, my pocket wriggled and jiggled as if there was something trying to get out. I took it out and there was a walking stone! It had grown two miniature legs from the two holes.

Next day I took my stone to school.
The teacher said, 'What have you brought in for show and tell?'
I had forgotten about show and tell, so I showed my stone. The children laughed as the stone walked around!
Then one child said, 'What did you call it?'
I replied, 'I haven't called it anything.'
He said, 'Call it Mr Stoney.'
I replied, 'Fine.'

In DT I finished early so the teacher suggested to make a bed for Mr Stoney, so I did.

It was home time and so I went home, I went to my mum and asked her, 'Can I keep this stone?'
'Yes,' said Mum.
It was late so I went to bed with Mr Stoney.

Rishi Patel (10)
Broadwater Primary School

MR STONEY'S BIG ADVENTURE

A few weeks ago I was walking along the beach and I tripped over a rather odd stone. It had quartz and it was smooth. I took it home, I didn't tell anyone I'd taken this pebble home. It was a secret!

A few weeks later I took the stone into school. At play time it was tickling me. I lifted up the stone - it had grown legs! I couldn't believe it. It even brought its own little brown schoolbag and it was wearing black shiny boots. I gave it to my teacher to look after so she would give it back at hometime.

At lunch the stone managed to jump out of the cupboard and run into my hands, he didn't want to go back.

The stone was my messenger. He sent messages. It was really fun. A few years past and the stone said, 'I miss my brother and sister stones. I want to go back.' I had a long think and decided to let him go. We were back at the beach. The stone was playing with his brother and sister stones and I never saw him have that much fun in his stoney little life!

Hania Naeem (10)
Broadwater Primary School

THE BRAVE HOBBIT

The quest was continued as I was walking along when suddenly this bag covered me, a voice which was quite familiar spoke. I thought it was . . .

'Where am I?' I asked.

Then a voice shouted, 'Give it to me, now!'

'What? You must have the wrong person, I have nothing valuable for anyone,' I said quietly.

'Don't lie, I know you, you have seven companions.'

'Seven companions? What are you talking about?'

'Don't lie Frodo Baggins!' he shouted.

'Huh, you must be . . .'

'Sarouman,' he sneered.

'Uh oh,' I said.

'Yes you are,' he laughed.

'Well, what do you want?' I asked.

'Well, two things: first your life, then the ring,' he replied.

'Never, actually you can't anyway,' I said.

'Don't lie to me, I know you are the ring bearer.'

'Gandalf has cast a spell on it.'

'That is not the rule of the ring,' he said.

'Got you now haven't I?' he chuckled.

'OK but first let me talk to my friends,' I said.

'I know what you're thinking of but it won't work,' he sniggered.

'Then let me out of this bag first,' I said demandingly.

'OK then,' he let me out of the bag and I was relieved. I looked around for an escape but we were at the highest floor. I had no chance to escape. Suddenly Gandalf appeared and used the sword that killed Saroun and stabbed Sarouman in his back. The crew was calling for me and Gandalf to escape and we did a run for it and that was the end of Sarouman. Phew!

'You should count yourself lucky,' Gandalf said.

'How did you know?' I asked.

'Well, we got some help from your old little friend,' he replied.

'Who?' I asked.

'Bilbo Baggins,' he replied.

'Really, how did he help?' I asked.

'He saw all of it, told us then we came straight here,' he replied.

'I am lucky,' I said.

Aqib Majid (10)
Broadwater Primary School

JOE AND THE SCARY CASTLE

Joe and his family decided to go and live in a big house in Devon. When they got there Joe was so excited.

That night Joe lay awake in his bed looking through his window at a crooked castle. It was dark outside so Joe could only see the outline. Joe lay wondering what it would be like to live in that castle. He expected it to be very creepy. Joe at last fell to sleep and had a nightmare. He dreamt he had gone to explore the castle and found lots of treasure but, when he thought he was safe a ghost jumped out of nowhere and Joe screamed and when he woke up he was sweating.

He sat up and looked at the clock on his side table. It was 7.47am. Joe got out of bed and walked over to his window. He stood there for a couple of minutes staring at the castle. He decided that very day to go and explore the castle. When Joe got all his things together he crept downstairs trying not to wake anyone.

About three quarters of an hour later Joe was standing in the doorway of the castle. He took one step inside the castle and the floorboard creaked. Joe jumped. As he jumped the door behind him shut. Joe had a look around. He went to open the door but it was locked. He went into the next room and the floor opened and he fell and once he'd hit the ground he ran home.

Katie Chapman (9)
Broadwater Primary School

MR STONEY'S BIG ADVENTURE

I was on a camel in Egypt when a light flashed at me. So I ran to the beach and started heading for the stone that was flashing at me. I picked it up and then it flashed again, it looked amazing! It looked so special it was speckled and it had quartz and the colour was pinkish with some brown and sort of white and grey spots. It was shaped like a flat sphere.

So I took it home with me and when I was on the boat I picked it up in my hands. Then I felt something move, I looked around, nothing there! So I opened my hand to see what was happening, I felt it again. It felt horrible! I looked under the stone. There were two tiny small pairs of legs. They felt funny but I got used to them.

Mr Stoney is my friend. He is a friendly stone, the best stone of all my collection.

I took him to school and told the class that our new guest was Mr Stoney. He was really shy. And by the time he got used to everyone it was the end of the day, he had a great time. We had literacy first thing, he found it very boring talking about nouns and adverbs. Of course he hasn't heard of nouns or adverbs before.

Then my teacher said, 'Why don't we have some stories - let our guest Mr Stoney go first as he has his hand up.'

So Mr Stoney told us all about when he got washed up in the Egyptian coast and how the waves made his skin smooth. He told brilliant jokes, but it was soon time to go home and everyone loved our new guest and told him to come back tomorrow.

Samantha Waters (10)
Broadwater Primary School

MR STONEY'S BIG ADVENTURE

It was Sunday and I felt like a stroll across the river. I found a stone, it could talk. I was so amazed by the stone so I had to pick it up, but then I dropped it. I took him home and got him ready for school tomorrow. There were these people at school that bullied me so I had to do something and fast!

Next day I went to school and everyone got on with my new best friend, Mr Stoney. It was swimming that day and he told everyone that he couldn't swim, but when he got in the water, he was off!

When we got to our class, Mr Stoney made all of the class laugh. He reminded us of Bobby Alvie because he left our school to go to a different country because he had brought a house there.

For lunch we had pasta. My friend Hania is a pasta fan.

Near the end of the day we had drama and Mr Stoney was very good at doing actions. He got a headteacher's award. So it was a very good day for my new friend, Mr Stoney.

Tianna Charles (10)
Broadwater Primary School

MR STONEY'S BIG ADVENTURE

One day I was on the beach and I saw a stone so I picked it up and I felt it. It was smooth and it was quartz.

When I got on the train and sat down, I held it gently and I realised it had legs. I looked at it carefully, I saw little eyes staring at me. Then I thought, *I'll put it next to me*, so I did and it started to walk.

When I got home I put it next to me in bed. It went to sleep.

The next day I took it to school and I put it in the next seat from me, where my friend sits. I told Hayden to sit with his friend. We all thought of a name for him, 'Mr Stoney' and we thought that was a nice name for him.

Mr Stoney learnt tons of facts. Every day he learns more, he becomes more intelligent. First of all he was a naughty stone, nowadays he's sensible. When it was lunchtime he ate crabs and mussels. When lunchtime was finished he had to learn maths. He had so much fun. When it was home time we had lots of fun.

Sharjeel Amjad (10)
Broadwater Primary School

MR STONEY'S BIG ADVENTURE

I was washing the dishes when I touched something solid. I drained the water and I saw a stone that had some white veins and had some pink colouring on it. I picked it up and put it flat on my hand. I took it up to my room and put it in my drawer.

I woke up the next morning quite early, about 4 o'clock. I opened the drawer and put the stone in my hand. Something tickled, I turned it over, it had legs!

I took him to school but when it was play time he had disappeared. He was the same colour as the ground! Then I saw him, a big bully from Year 6 was just about to step on Mr Stoney, but I ran over just in time. I got him but the bully saw Mr Stoney.
He called Mr Stoney by saying, 'Hey you stupid stone!'
Mr Stoney told me to hold him next to his face so I did.
'My name is Mr Stoney.'
I saw that Mr Stoney had grown a mouth.
He said, 'Your name calling will never hurt me.'

From that day on, the bully never hurt a fly, and I took Mr Stoney home and played with him like a best friend. The bully ended up doing ballet and always wore pink!

Shahzadi Khan (10)
Broadwater Primary School

MY STONEY BECOMING MORTAL

I was walking along a beach. I found a greyish-silver star-shaped stone.
I picked it up and it started to talk to me.
It said, 'My name is Mr Stoney.'

We went to school together and I used it for show and tell. Everyone
liked my star-shaped stone, but when it was pitch-black at night it
started to glow and twinkle like the stars and the moon. All of a sudden
it had some words which started to appear. The words said, 'I shall give
you the power to fly! So you will be led to the mountain of life so I can
show you that I'm supposed to be in mortal form.'

The stone gave me the power to fly and we flew and got to the top of
the mountain of life and he turned into a human.
A voice said, 'If you do not give a soul to Mr Stoney in 48 hours he
shall perish to another dimension.'
I said, 'How will I get his soul back?'
He said, 'By counting up to ten.'
I felt really silly.
All of a sudden the voice said, 'Count now!'
I did and Mr Stoney's soul came back to him.

Al-Haya Minhas (10)
Broadwater Primary School

MR STONEY'S BIG ADVENTURE

I was on a trip with my class at the beach when I found a stone. I picked it up, I touched it, it was so smooth. The waves had gone over and over it. It was white with grey freckles on it. It had a blush of pink, the pink on it caught my eye. It also had a shade of brown. It looked over a thousand years old. It had veins on it which were called quartz. It had got the quartz because while the Earth's crust was forming, all the stones squashed together and that's how the quartz was formed.

I decided to take it to school, so I put it in my pocket. It was the end of my trip and we all sat in the coach. I took the stone out of my pocket and held it tightly in my hand. Suddenly I felt a tickly thing on my hand, it tickled again!

I looked under the stone and found it had legs! Two little tiny legs. I put it back into my pocket. I thought I should name it Mr Stoney. I showed it to my friends Hania and Tianna. They told me to show it to Miss Woolridge. Miss Woolridge was surprised to see it.

We had literacy and Mr Stoney learned how to write poems. He played with us. My teacher asked me what his name was.
I said, 'Mr Stoney!'
He walked up the stairs with me to the classroom. He has been going to school since then and it's always with me.

Noor Razaq (10)
Broadwater Primary School

SHORT STORY

There was once a boy called Billy and he had bright blue eyes, short ginger hair and was a kind little boy.

One day, Billy woke up, brushed his teeth and had his breakfast. He felt really bored as his brother had gone to a football match. He thought and thought, suddenly he had an idea. He could invite some friends over to have a picnic. He called three friends over, Lily, Jake and Paul. They all brought some food to share. Lily brought some grapes, Jake brought some chocolate and Paul brought some strawberries and cream. Billy's mum had made some jam sandwiches and fairy cakes. She brought some biscuits and some drinks as well.

They had started to eat when spits of rain came falling down. They thought it would be alright but it got worse so they brought the food in and were very unhappy.

Luckily, Mum had already put a cloth down in the front room just in case it did rain, so it was alright after all. All the food got finished and everyone was full.

That day Billy said to his friends, 'Well, why don't you lot stay at my house, so it will be a sleepover?'
They had planned to have a midnight feast, but no one got up.

It had been a fun day and everyone enjoyed it.

Sabahut Beg (9)
Broadwater Primary School

MR STONEY'S BIG ADVENTURE

Once I went to a beach. I was swimming in the sea. When I came out something hit me on my feet. When I looked down I saw a stone. I liked the stone, so I picked it up. It was grey with white dots. It looked very old. It had cracks on one side and a bit of pink on it. Then it was time to go home. I took the stone with me and I thought of a name. I called it Mr Stoney.

On the way home I was holding my stone. I felt something moving. When I looked at the stone, it had grown little legs.

The next day, when I went to school, the stone walked behind me. I showed Mr Stoney to my friends, but did not tell anything about him. He was about a million years old. I went on a magic journey with him. I could know things that happened a million years ago. It was very fun and some of it was very scary. I told everyone about Mr Stoney's adventure.

Mr Stoney is my best friend. I like Mr Stoney. He makes my work easier for me because some of the things I don't know, Mr Stoney knows instead!

Soniya Ghani (10)
Broadwater Primary School

RISE OF THE DEAD

A long time ago in a faraway house, lived three children. Their names were Joe, Jack and Bill. One Hallowe'en night, they wanted to do something other than go trick or treating.

'Why don't we go to Spook Street?' asked Jack, the oldest boy.

Bill and Joe gasped. Spooky Street was very scary in the light, so they didn't want to go in the dark. It wasn't the street that was scary, it was the house number 13.

This was a haunted house. Many years before, a young lady was murdered in the house. The murderer had never been caught and even now neighbours could hear her cry and scream.

'It will be fun!' said Jack.

Bill was the youngest and was very scared. 'I don't want to go,' he said.

'Chicken, chicken . . . Bill is a girl! He's so scared!' said the other two.

Just to prove them wrong, Bill said he would go.

All the children went to spy on the house. They camped in the house and opened the door and switched on the lamp. *Squeak, squeak, squeak.*

'What was that noise?' asked Bill.

'Let's go out, please man, let's go.'

'Oh my . . .'

'What? What is it!'

'It's a dead . . . rat!' said Jack.

'Eurgh, eurgh, eurgh! That is disgusting, that is sick!' Joe and Bill said.

Squeak went the door. The door opened and there came in the man with a knife killing everyone. The children jumped, so scared that they ran as fast as they could. They ran away and will never go back!

Gurpreet Gill (10)
Broadwater Primary School

MR STONEY'S BIG ADVENTURE

Hello! My name is Mr Stoney. I have been washed onto the beach. I'm sixty-five years old and a girl took me home to London. I'm surrounded by freckles and I'm growing two little feet. I was a very sad stone, but now I'm quite happy.

The girl went to school the next day. She was my girlfriend so I went with her. She started to feel my cold shell so she noticed that I was sitting on her shoe and biting her feet. When she came home she took a peek and then saw me cleaning her shoe.

The next day she took me to school. She told her class that I was funny so the people liked me. They made me pass notes in class. They even made me eat the goldfish who was cute. They learned that I missed the sea. I shared stories about my old mate, Sir Walter Rayleigh, who made me walk the plank, it wasn't really bad. At the end of the day we played football and from then on I've never been lonely again!

Ila Magdaong (10)
Broadwater Primary School

MR STONEY'S BIG ADVENTURE

In Mauritius I was walking on the beach. It was really hot. I hadn't walked too far when I saw a pretty, smooth, grey-speckled white stone, so I took it home. I held the stone tightly. I felt something stretching out of the stone and when I looked at the stone, I saw two sticks. *That's strange*, I thought. I then went to sleep.

The next day I was going to school. I saw my stone walking next to me. I just couldn't believe that my stone could walk. He walked around the hall and jumped up and down the stairs. When the stone got to the classroom, he got ready for science like the other children.

At lunchtime the stone jumped onto my plate and ate some of my dinner with me. After lunchtime the stone got so confident at maths by sitting with Sandy and learning.

At home time, the stone was not bothered about walking home with me, so I just ran off with my friends. I forgot about the stone so the stone had to sleep in the pencil pot.

The next day when the children came in the class the stone was still sleeping. Everybody was getting ready for work so everybody took their pencils out. A boy called Jack saw the stone on his pencil so he put it in his pocket and took it home. I was worried about the stone. When I went home I looked everywhere but I still couldn't find the stone. When the stone woke up, he jumped out of Jack's pocket and ran to my house. I was so happy.

I said, 'My stone is back, you're my best stone ever - the great Mr Stone.'

Binesh Habib (10)
Broadwater Primary School

CONFUSION

Ray Baker is a person who is scared of nothing at all. He thinks he is so tough and strong, but he soon finds out that he's not.

'Bye Mum, I am going to school now,' Ray said to his mum.
'OK love, have you got your lunch?' questioned his mum.
There was no reply. Ray had already left.

When he arrived at school, he saw the girl that he liked. He tried to impress her by doing triple flips, but nothing ever worked. Her name was Pricilla McAllistair. She was the most popular girl in the whole school. When all the children got in the classroom, their class teacher, Mr Richardson, asked for their homework. Ray never did his homework and he was always getting punished. Mrs McFreeman, the headmistress, was fed up with Ray always going to her office because, firstly, she would always end up with a sore throat, and, secondly, he never listened.

Today Ray didn't go to Mrs McFreeman's office, she came to the classroom.
'Class, since I don't have the energy to think of a punishment for Ray, would you like to do the honours of kindly picking a punishment for him?' asked Mrs McFreeman, sounding very tired.
Pricilla put her hand up. Ray got a bit worried because she was the only one in the class who had brilliant ideas.
'Yes Pricilla?' said Mrs McFreeman.
'How about if he spends a night or two at the dreaded house,' suggested Pricilla.
'What an excellent idea!' exclaimed both Mr Richardson and Mrs McFreeman.
Ray wasn't too pleased about this because whoever went in there never came out. That night he started to pack his bags. He couldn't sleep at all. He had never been scared in his life.

As he was leaving in the morning, he started to shake non-stop. He arrived at the house at about 6pm, so it was quite dark. He couldn't reach the door handle because it was ridiculously high up. Ray soon opened the door and once he got inside he wished that he had always done his homework. A chill ran up his spine as he walked through the dark corridors.

As he strolled into the first room, he felt a bit uneasy. Everything around him started to spiral and twist, the walls seemed to change and it seemed as if he was in a different room. He was very confused. The door changed colour and he started to hear strange noises. There was a scuttling in the floorboards then a strong wind blowing and howling. Ray wished he had brought his Game Boy to take his mind off things. He left the room feeling queasy and went to have a wander.

There were worn out paintings and old-fashioned carpets. There was a musty smell. He heard a howling and thought he saw a white figure in the distance. A chill ran up his spine once again. His feet went into automatic and he started running. He tried to stop himself but he just kept on and on.

Ray stopped in front of a tall dark door. He opened it even though he didn't want to. It was as if someone or something had taken over him. In this room was a tall grandfather clock, just standing there motionless. On the ground lay a corpse of a small child. As Ray bent down to take a look at the corpse, the eyelids suddenly opened. Ray couldn't move because of the way that the child looked at him.
'Please don't hurt me,' Ray squealed.
'Oh, I am not going to hurt you, I am simply going to scare you to death,' said the child in a hauntingly scary voice.
This time Ray intended to run but his legs were still. 'That's it, I have had enough!' shouted Ray. He started running and running until he stopped at the same door he had come into the corridor from, but it looked very different. The colour had changed from brown to red, the pattern had vanished and the knob was bronze and not silver.

It seemed very familiar and then he remembered that it was the same door as the one at the entrance. He took a chance and opened it, trembling with fear. 'Yes!' Ray screamed. It was fresh air at last.

Ray ran all the way home and it was only then that he realised that he had reached the door handle up at the house. He had forgotten about the business up at the house and said sorry for not doing his homework. From that day on he always did his homework.

Amaya Pitharas (10)
Our Lady Of Lourdes RC Primary School

THE MYSTERY OF THE CYCLOPS

One foggy, wet afternoon, Polly Weecap was in the house watching TV. Polly was 76 years old. She didn't realise that there were funny noises upstairs. After about three or four hours, Polly went upstairs to go to bed. She put her pyjamas on, but heard a voice.

It said, 'Polly, why are you not in your bed? It's way past deathtime! Ha! Ha! Ha!'

Polly didn't go to bed, she put pillows under the duvet. Polly hid in the cupboard.

All of a sudden, the door swung open. Polly looked out of a gap in the cupboard. She figured it was a man. He had a knife. He stabbed the pillows. Then he turned and stabbed Polly through the gap in the cupboard.

This is what was believed to have happened, but nobody knows what really did happen. Some people think it was the Cyclops of death. It's a mystery!

Molly Lockwood (9)
Our Lady Of Lourdes RC Primary School

THE MYSTERY OF THE VAMPIRE

One day when I was walking to school, I heard a scream in my friend's house. I ran in and saw her with blood pouring down. I rang the ambulance and they took her to the hospital. I was crying because she died. She was my best friend. I told everyone at school but they didn't care. Only one person cared and that was her sister. She was crying every day. I felt sorry for her.

I went to the hospital and asked how she died. They said something bit her. They found a piece of a tooth in her neck. They said that it was not an animal tooth, it was a human's tooth. It was a very sharp tooth.

I went to get Jemma, my best friend's sister. I showed her the tooth. She said that it looked like a vampire's fang.
Then I thought. I said, 'Of course it's a vampire's tooth. Who else drinks blood?' I took it to the hospital and said to them that it was a vampire tooth.

On the Thursday that I went to school, I heard the scream. I heard a person speaking in my ear, it was someone who didn't like Jemma. I knew that person would kill Jemma. I knew I must get Jemma. I ran to Jemma's house but it was too late, he'd taken her somewhere. I was really scared. I thought the man was after me, but then if he was after me, then why didn't he say he would kill me? I heard another scream and ran to where it was coming from. I saw Jemma and she was bleeding from the arm. I took her to the hospital. Luckily she didn't die.

A week later, Jemma came out of hospital. She was really scared so I let her come to my house. I walked into my house.
My mum asked me, 'Where have you been today? I was really worried about you.'
'Sorry Mum, I was in hospital with Jemma.'

'Why was Jemma in hospital?'
'She was in hospital because she's broken her arm.'
'Is she alright?'
'She will be. Is it OK if she stays with us?'
'Of course!' said Mum.

Gina Christopher (9)
Our Lady Of Lourdes RC Primary School

MELTED SATAN

One day Satan made a crystal ball to watch Earth. He saw a little boy and his name was Kai. Kai wasn't scared of anything, but Satan knew it. Satan wanted Kai to be his royal scarer king, to be tough and scare or kill bad people or good people.

Satan sent a messenger to try to get Kai. The Devil's messenger went to Earth dressed as a boy.
He went to Kai and said, 'Please come here. I want to be your friend and talk to you.'
'Sure kid, whatever, I'll talk to you and be your friend,' replied Kai.
'Thanks Kai,' the new kid said to Kai.
'Hey,' Kai said, 'how do you know my name?'
'I'm taking you to Hell,' said the little boy. 'Ha, ha!'
A big *boom* came and Kai and the little boy went to Satan.
Satan said, 'I give you the opportunity to be my royal scarer, to scare and kill people.'
Kai said, 'Yes, only if you do what I want and if I have power and don't kill good people.'
'Deal!' Satan said.

Kai went in a little girl's house and scared her. The girl fainted in bed. Kai scared 50 girls and 20 boys. Satan was laughing. Kai met 3 people and they said to him, 'Do you want to be in our team?'
Kai said, 'I'd love to.'
They all went to see Satan.
Kai said, 'The deal is off.' He joined the other three people in the team.

Katherine Tobin (9)
Our Lady Of Lourdes RC Primary School

THE MISSING CHILDREN

Once on a dark and stormy night, a girl moved into a haunted house, but she knew it was haunted and was terrified. The girl's name was Molly.

On the second night she went out with her friend, Suzanna, into a forest. Halfway there they screamed and died with horror. The only things that were left were their eyeballs, front teeth and blood.

Since then, nobody has ever been in that forest ever again and they never knew what or who did it . . .

Alejandra Gomez (9)
Our Lady Of Lourdes RC Primary School

ROMANCE BLOOMS

There once lived a prince called Diego, the son of Sameto VI and Queen Hianan. He was a child that had everything when he was growing up. He was a teenager that started a trend and finished it, but as a growing man of 22 years of age, all he wanted now was a girl that brightened up his day, made his heart stop because of her beauty and would make a lovely bride and mother, but for now he remained single.

On the other side of the town there lived a young girl whose only dream was to have a man whisk her away from her current life of being a maid for the spoilt rotten children of the Vasgezs. Catheliene was an only child that was badly treated, then taken to an orphanage at the age of 2. She was then adopted by the Vasgezs and until the twins were born, she had been treated fine.

As the day grew on, Diego decided to take a walk to the town. Catheliene was shopping in the market, trying to find some meat for the Vasgezs' dinner. As Diego crossed the road, he found himself stood in front of the most beautiful girl he had ever seen. As Catheliene realised who he was, she ran as fast as she could. Diego ran after her.
'Do you believe in love at first sight?' asked the prince.
Catheliene just looked into Diego's eyes and said, 'Yes, I do.'
'Then come with me,' replied Diego.

Catheliene dropped her bags and walked with Diego to the beach where the dolphins elegantly swam and the doves gracefully flew. As the sun set, Catheliene suddenly realised that she was going to be late to cook the dinner for the twins.
'I have to go. I hope I see you again.'

As Catheliene was leaving, Diego soon realised; what if he didn't see her again? And decided not to let go of her. Diego finally let go of Catheliene and said, 'As long as I live I will always love you.'
Catheliene walked off into the sunlight.

Diego never did see Catheliene again, but that one day he spent with her was enough to last a lifetime.

Erin O'Garro (11)
Our Lady Of Lourdes RC Primary School

THE CASE OF THE TALKING TROUSERS

One day, Wesley promised Foxy and Jamal he would go and see the match that started at 2pm with them. When he was eating he saw the clock. It was 1.58pm. He was late. He'd have to go to the river bank.

When he was going to the river bank he looked at the clock. 1.47pm. He said, 'Now I am early!' He heard a noise. It was someone's old trousers talking.
The trousers said, 'I have a train to catch.'
Wesley took them to the station.

Meanwhile, Foxy and Jamal were on the river bank. Wesley wasn't there. Foxy and Jamal heard someone shouting for help from the river. It was a man. The man has rescued a dog but he couldn't find his trousers. Foxy and Jamal could only find a T-shirt for the man, but it was pink and fluffy.

The man thanked Foxy and Jamal anyway. The man said, 'I am Frank.'

At the train station, Wesley had noticed that the trousers didn't speak anymore.

Frank went to the police station. He said, 'Someone's got my trousers.'

Wesley noticed the name in the trousers. 'Write, Frank'. Wesley went to meet Foxy and Jamal.
Foxy said, 'Those are Frank's.'
They gave them to Frank. Frank thanked Foxy, Jamal and Wesley.

Antonio Furchi (9)
Our Lady Of Lourdes RC Primary School

LOST IN THE WOOD

One night a boy was in his nanny's house in his bed and he shared a bedroom with his sister. They were staying the week and had been there for four days. They lived a long way from their nanny's. Their mum and dad were there too.

The next day Jake, the boy, and his sister called Liz, went to the woods without their parents knowing. Their parents always said not to go in the woods if it was too dark, but they never listened to them. They went too far and they were lost in the wood.

They were worried that they would never see their parents again. Jake was really tired, and so was Liz. They were crying because they wouldn't see their mum and dad ever again. Their parents were going to forget they were lost. They had to spend the night in the wood.

Back home where their nanny lived, their parents had phoned the police and they were looking everywhere. Their parents were terrified.

A policeman called Sam went in the wood. He had found the children and walked them to their nanny's house. As soon as they saw their mum and dad, they ran to them, and their nanny too. Their mum and dad said thank you to the policeman.

Eleanor O'Sullivan (8)
Our Lady Of Lourdes RC Primary School

THE STORY OF MURDER MANOR

You know that house on the highest hill of the highest mountain? Well, like many things, that house has a story, a story that made people believe it was haunted! I am Joeanna and I am one of the few people who went in the house and came out alive! I will tell you the story, it is the story of Murder Manor.

It all began on a cold, misty night. Me and my best friend, Becky, had just come back for a party. It was so dark and misty that we had to stop off at the nearest house, yes Murder Manor.

The manor was a horrid, dark place. We were lucky to find candles and matches so we could find our way around. Becky, being stupid as always, went to put her coat in one of the closets. Just as she opened the door, a human body (that had probably just been slaughtered) fell down on top of her, knocking her to the ground!

Once she had seen what had fallen on her, she screamed for dear life. I ran as fast as I could to see what was wrong. I flung the body off her and grabbed her hand and we both ran up the stairs. We were halfway up the stairs when we heard an unusual noise. It got louder and louder until we heard a *clump, clump* coming up the stairs. We ran into the nearest room and hid under the bed.

The thumping noise soon stopped. Me and Becky felt quite safe until a shadow of a bony hand appeared. I turned away.
'Help!' yelled Becky.
I turned around to save her, but I was too late. She was gone. Whatever was there had taken her. I wanted to go out and save her but I was too scared.

About 15 minutes later, I came out from under the bed to start looking for Becky. As I came out of the room, I saw Becky's jacket on the floor. It was covered in blood. I just walked past it. I started walking down the stairs, when, *clump, clump, clump.* I ran for my life as soon as I heard that. I kicked the door open and ran out.

As soon as I got home I told my parents but they didn't believe me. I hope you did, for that was the story of Murder Manor!

Danielle O'Brien (11)
Our Lady Of Lourdes RC Primary School

THE WOOLPACK

One Sunday morning it was a special day for me. It was my Holy Communion party. It was going to be a big party. Everybody was going to it. I was so excited I couldn't wait. But first we had to go to Mass.

Afterwards we were going to a pub called The Woolpack. It had a pool table. They had a game - 'Spot The Difference'. I got ready for Mass. Then we went to the church and went to communion.

Afterwards we went to the hall. There were two tables full of food. We had lunch. Then we went to The Woolpack. We had a couple of games of pool and 'Spot The Difference'. Then I had a drink and then went home. Then I watched a bit of TV. Then I had a bowl of cereal and went to bed.

Harry Legg (8)
Our Lady Of Lourdes RC Primary School

THE MAGICAL PARTY

There was a girl called Josy. It was her party. She had a sleepover party. First they played outside then they went to the park. They played near the pond. Then they went home. Mollie arrived, she was fat so no one played with her. They had cake, Coke, sweets, sandwiches and lots of other things. Then people's mums and dads came to take them home.

The people who stayed to sleep had more fun. Josy had a hat that was magic. She'd asked her friends what they all wanted. They said money. She got £200 which they all shared between them. It was a fantastic party.

Maria Cherchi (8)
Our Lady Of Lourdes RC Primary School

THE HULK FIGHTS HARRY POTTER

Once there lived The Hulk and Harry Potter. The Hulk was green and very strong. Harry Potter was a wizard. He was very powerful. His wand was very strong.

The Hulk was walking through a pond and suddenly Harry Potter appeared from nowhere! The Hulk said, 'Well, well, well, we meet again.'
Then Harry Potter said, 'You're useless.'
Then The Hulk punched Harry, so Harry used the spell, 'Flipendo', but The Hulk kicked and punched as hard as he could, then Harry Potter, the strongest kid-wizard died.

At the church everybody was crying. Everyone had their tissues out. Harry's auntie was there but she didn't care. At the party Harry Potter's auntie left. Then Harry's cake came. It was a Hogwarts-shaped cake because that was where he'd learned his spells. It was his favourite place.

Chris Lefteris Pitharas (8)
Our Lady Of Lourdes RC Primary School

THE HORROR SCHOOL

I'm Emma and I go to Our Lady Of Lourdes School. My school is just plain white. I really want to get a bit of paint splattered on the walls, but the problem is the teachers stay up late, like about 10 o'clock at night.

It was my best friend, Eleanor's birthday. She was 8 and was having a sleepover party. She said I was definitely invited to her party.

On Thursday the sleepover came. First we played Connect 4. It was great. Eleanor had a brother who was 18 years old. He was called Simon. Next we played a drawing competition. Simon was the judge, I won. Then we played dares. Eleanor dared me to go to school and paint the walls, so I did.

When I got to school, I started to paint the school in yellow and pink paint. There was howling and suddenly I shrivelled up into a ball, then there was a scream and a shout, so I screamed. I heard my friends giggling. It was a set up! Then the teacher came and we all got detention.

Joseph Ope (7)
Our Lady Of Lourdes RC Primary School

LIKE ZOLA

One day my dad bought tickets to see Chelsea play. Me, my dad and Matthew were going. We got there by train, it took 2 hours to get there.

When we got there we were early so we got a hot dog with tomato ketchup. We sat down in our seats and the match soon began.

Straight away Chelsea scored, it was 1-0. Zola was the scorer. At half-time it was still 1-0 to Chelsea. At half-time a lucky fan has to have a match with Zola and I got called out to play against him.

The referee blew his whistle for the match to start. The referee said, 'You have 1 minute.' When one minute was over I'd won 4-0.

Chelsea won 3-0 against Arsenal. After the match Zola said to the manager, 'Can Ryan play for the team?'
He said, 'Yes, sure he can!'

My first match was against Man U, I scored 2 goals, John Terry scored 1. We won 3-0. We were top and I got man of the match. At the end of the season we came first in the league. I got top goal scorer with 41 goals and Real Madrid, Barcelona and AC Milan wanted me but I said, 'I'm staying here.'

On my first game of the new season I got tickets for all of my family and I scored 2 goals!

Ryan Murphy (9)
Our Lady Of Lourdes RC Primary School

A Scary, Ghost Story

Hello, my name is Luke. Now I will tell you about the scariest story that's ever been told. This is my story.

One day I was walking down the street with my friends.
'Oooooooh! Oooooooh!'
Oh shut up! Who is telling this story? Me! Now where was I? Oh yeah
. . .

We went into a spooky library. We were all hoping to see the dinosaurs. When we went to see the museum, it was old and crooked. Inside were fish. Fish! Fish! Fish! In fact all the museum was, was fish. We went to the front of the museum and found out that the door was locked. (I frightened you there didn't I? Don't worry, the scary part isn't now . . . or is it? Stop shaking.) Wait I see something.
'Oooooooh.'
A ghost, run for your life.
Then the ghost said, 'It's a joke!'

Luke Dowling (9)
Our Lady Of Lourdes RC Primary School

THE HORRIBLE TASK

'Alan, Alan, wake up,' shouted Uncle Fred.

'What's the matter?' moaned Alan.

'It's Mum, she disappeared near the computer. She typed her name (Monica) on the computer and she vanished.'

'Get lost!' said Alan grumpily, so Uncle Fred kicked him out of bed.

He took his pyjamas off slowly and went to the study. He typed his mum's name and the computer flashed and he disappeared too.

He woke up again with a shock. He saw his mum, or did he . . . ? And where were they?

Daniele Boeri (9)
Our Lady Of Lourdes RC Primary School

THE PRINCESS AND PRINCE'S SECRETS

Once there lived a family of ghosts who liked to haunt. One night a princess was sitting by the fire trying to keep warm, she heard a noise so she ran to see her father and mother. The princess told her father that she'd heard a ghost but she hadn't seen him.

The next day she saw them and became a good friend of theirs. When she got married she kept the secret to herself and she didn't tell a soul.

One day the secret was ruined, she told the prince, but he said he didn't mind because he had a secret too. His secret was that he could speak to snakes and that he had a witch dog whose name was Sparkie.

The princess's name was Witney and the prince's name was Liam and they were in love. They went to the pet shop to try and get a dog but they couldn't decide whether to get a cat, a fish or a dog so they got all three.

Two months later Witney gave birth to a boy and a girl, they were so cute. Liam said that he would name the boy and she would name the girl. He named the boy John and she named the girl Tammy. They were a happy family until one day the prince wanted to leave to go to America, but that's another story.

Tammy Quintin (9)
Our Lady Of Lourdes RC Primary School

666 THE DEVIL'S NUMBER

It was a wet, foggy Monday morning, Molly, Ivet, Julia and Emily had been in the car for 3 hours. Finally the car stopped. They got out of the car. They were looking for a new house.

There was an old woman at the gate, her name was Cinzia, she had a kind husband, his name was Danny. They were there to open the gate. Cinzia opened the gate when suddenly Danny screamed, 'Don't go in, it's evil.' Cinzia put her hand over his mouth. She began to laugh, 'Don't believe him he's a bit loopy.'

They walked through the gate then Emily began to scream. Emily and Julia were sisters, when they were 9 or 10 they were in a crash, both their parents had died. Emily has a mental problem and Julia gets scared easily. Julia looked at the door number '666'. Julia jumped around shouting, 'The Devil's number.'

Molly stepped in first. *Crash!* Molly went flying through the floorboards. The other girls went down to help her up. There was a big red chest so they opened it. In it there was a book and as soon as they opened the book it let out a tremendous scream.

That night Emily got in a bit of a fit, she kept saying, 'Fireplace.' Molly left her and began to walk upstairs. Suddenly she froze. There on the wall written in blood was *The fireplace*. Behind her Molly heard deep breathing.

Next morning Molly had gone. They checked the whole house, but for some reason they couldn't find her and in the end they all forgot.

A few days later Julia had to send Emily to her room. A few hours later Julia and Ivet went to the garden. Emily was tied to a pole and was dead. Suddenly Julia found it hard to breathe and collapsed.

'Now I have you alone,' said a voice.

Ivet ran and fell through the floorboards. Molly's dead body was lying on the floor. Ivet got out of the hole and ran out of the house.

A few years later Ivet had a home, she looked out the window and saw a very white hand . . .

Emily McCabe (9)
Our Lady Of Lourdes RC Primary School

THE SECRET GETAWAY

Boop, boop, boop, went Katie's alarm clock. 'Another morning of another horrible school day,' she sighed. Katie got out of bed and heard her mum on the phone. She managed to work out a little of the conversation. Something about money problems and moving out. 'Oh no,' she cried, 'we could be moving house!' Katie tried to get dressed as quickly as she could and ran downstairs.

'Who was that?' Katie asked her mum.
'Ermmm . . . what are you having for your breakfast?' she said. Knowing her mum was trying to change the subject Katie just said, 'Frosties,' and ran off into the living room.

Katie switched on the TV and began to wonder what was really going to happen to her. Suddenly all her surroundings had changed and she was stuck in a strange world.
'How strange,' she said, 'I wonder where I am?' She walked over and found a passageway, she ran down trying to find a way out, but it was no use.
'Help, I'm trapped,' cried a voice.
'Where?' shouted Katie.
'Down here.'
Katie ran towards the voice and found two people sitting down on the ground.
'Free us, please,' they cried. Katie ran towards them and untied them.
'Hi, my name is Julia and his name is Ryan. We've been trapped in here for years! Anyhow, how did you get down here?'
'I don't know. I was just . . . here,' Katie said.
'Weird,' Ryan said.
Katie ran towards a door in front of her and entered with Ryan and Julia.
'Aarrgghh,' screamed Julia and Katie and suddenly Katie was at home with Ryan on her left and Julia on her right watching TV.

Cinzia Leonard (9)
Our Lady Of Lourdes RC Primary School

JOSH'S DREAM

One day my dad bought a couple of tickets for a hockey match, Blue Eagles vs Knights. I supported the team Blue Eagles. We went into the stadium, it was a long way up the stairs. When we got there the stadium had hardly any people there.

The ref blew his whistle, Knights started. 1-0 to Knights. Blue Eagles got the ball back, 2-1 to Blue Eagles.

At the end of the match Blue Eagles won 6-2. I was sitting in section 2, row 10, seat 4. They had a lucky dip on the pitch. It was section 2, row 10, seat . . . 4! 'Yes!' I said and jumped up in surprise. The prize was taking 3 penalties. I took the first one, 'Goal!' Second one, 'Goal!' Third, rebound, 'Goal!' I saw the coach after the game, he said to me, 'Do you want to be part of our team?'
'Yes,' I replied.

The first time I played for Blue Eagles was on 26th October 2002, I scored 10 goals. In all of the games I played in I scored 10 goals, apart from the last game I had, the Cup Final, I scored 5 goals, but we still won.

First half I scored 2 goals and Michael scored 2. It was 4-2. I scored my last 3 goals. 'Time,' shouted the ref.

Joshua Wood (9)
Our Lady Of Lourdes RC Primary School

THE NEWBORN BABY

One miserable evening the Beck family were watching TV. The children were upstairs in Amy's room. The adults (Jack and Maria) were downstairs watching TV.

Jack said to his wife Maria, 'I think we shall tell the children that you are going to have a bab . . .' Before Jack could say the rest of the word he was interrupted by the ring of the phone. *Ring, ring.*

Maria picked it up, it was her friend Susie.

Susie said, 'Have you told your children that you're going to have a baby?'

Maria replied, 'No, not yet, I am going to tell them now.'

'OK, bye.'

Jack called the children down.

Gemma said, 'What do you want?'

Maria said, 'I want to tell you something special.'

Jack then said very slowly, 'Your mother is going to have a baby.'

The children were so, so excited and surprised.

Charlie said, 'Is it a boy or a girl?'

Maria replied, 'I don't know, I need to have four or five scans. Right off to bed, it's nine o'clock.'

The next day the children were writing boys' names and girls' names and Maria and Jack were talking about where the baby would sleep. Maria suggested the baby could sleep in their room and then it could sleep in Amy's room but if it was a boy it could sleep in Charlie's room.

A month later Maria kept getting pains in her stomach, she went to hospital.

The doctors and nurses said, 'You are going to have the baby now.'

'Can I call Jack?'

'Yes of course.'

When Jack got the message he came rushing up to the hospital. When he arrived Maria was having the baby. Maria had a baby girl, then they went home happily together.

Elisa Mariani (9)
Our Lady Of Lourdes RC Primary School

LOVE STORY

Faraway from here were a group of boys and girls in Spain. Their names were Sean, Matthew and Sol, then there were the girls, Emma, Catherine, Erin and a beautiful young lady with blonde straight hair and nice legs, all us boys liked her but the only boy she liked was Matthew.

The next day we went to the beach and Sean and Emma confessed to the group they loved each other. Everyone in the group was screaming, 'I'm so happy for you two.' Then the girls stayed behind talking about Emma and Sean.

Us boys were talking about Mariah Carey and about how I thought she loved me and then I hit the ground, the woman of my dreams was there, she said. 'Hello.'
'Uh, uh, uh, hello.'
All my friends were asking her out for me and she said she'd love to so we started going out.

A few years later me, Matthew, married Mariah Carey and had the best life. We lived in a mansion and had 10 children. Sean and Emma had been married for 11 years and had 9 children and were expecting another. We all lived a great life, except Sean and Emma didn't have a nice house because it was a flat and their car was a Fiat. Me and Mariah had a swimming pool and tennis courts. Catherine and Sol became our slaves. We did have Erin as well but we kicked her out. We had a happy life.

Matthew Murphy (11)
Our Lady Of Lourdes RC Primary School

THE VERY SCARY NIGHT

One very dark night when Mollie stopped playing with her hospital kit she started to watch 'The Mummy Returns' with her brother Scott. It was a very dark night. Mollie had her pyjamas on. They weren't allowed to watch it. Mollie was ten and Scott was nine. Children over fifteen could watch it. The babysitter fell asleep and started to sleepwalk home. They started to have Coca-Cola and popcorn.

Mollie fell asleep halfway through it. She slept on the sofa. When Scott went upstairs he saw Mollie's hospital kit, he thought for a moment, then he said to himself, 'Maybe I could use her bandages and dress up as 'The Mummy Returns'.

Scott started to put the bandages on him. He got a bit tangled so he called his friend Peter. He said, 'Come round and help me dress up as a mummy. don't knock I'll wait outside.'

When Peter had helped he went home. When he slammed the door Mollie woke up. Scott ran downstairs and scared Mollie.
Mollie screamed, 'Argh, argh, there's a mummy in the house.' Then she saw it was her bandages and her parents came in. They were then sent to bed. They were never allowed to watch it again.

Christina Frutuoso (8)
Our Lady Of Lourdes RC Primary School

KING BECKHAM AND THE MAN UTD TOUCH

King Beckham banged his head against Finnan when Man Utd played Liverpool. Beckham ran at Finnan to start a fight. Beckham pushed Finnan and Finnan had a Man Utd strip. Finnan took a free kick for Man Utd. Goal! Finnan scored a free kick. Man Utd won the cup. Champions! Beckham had the Premiership Cup, the fans were really drunk. Soon after every person in Great Britain played for Man Utd. The whole nation was supporting Man Utd.

But the next day Ronaldo played for Real Madrid, Riisie played for Liverpool, van Nistelrooy went to Barcelona and Fergie left Manchester United and went to Manchester City. Jermanie Jenas went to Arsenal Football Club. James Beattie went to Sunderland, Poyet went to Crystal Palace and Sheringham went to Portsmouth FC. Beckham was doomed!

Ryan Delaney (8)
Our Lady Of Lourdes RC Primary School

HARRY POTTER AND THE CHAMBER OF SECRETS

Once upon a time there were two boys called Harry Potter and Ron Weasley and a girl called Hermione Granger. She was a clever girl but the boys were so dumb that they always got things wrong because they didn't always go to the library.

But one day when Harry was about to play Quidditch they had to cancel it because Hermione was frozen and they had to get Ron because she was so, so, so important to them.

But when she was frozen Ron and Harry found something in Hermione's hand, it was something from a book. It said, 'If you want to live don't look into my eyes and to keep me alive you must go to the library and do your own homework!'

Katerina Paraschou (7)
Our Lady Of Lourdes RC Primary School

THE COFFIN WITH A BLACK HOLE

Lila and Catriona were sisters. Lila was 18 and Catriona was 14. One day Lila, Catriona and their family went on a camping trip to Devon. Lila and her family went on an exploring trip in the woods without Catriona. Catriona went to Kent's Cavern and had a really great time there. On her way back she saw a rubbish dump which scared her. She ran back to the camp site. She persuaded Lila to go back to the dump with her.

After searching they saw a coffin with a skull engraved on the lid. Suddenly the top of the coffin opened and *shalam* the ghost appeared and said, 'My children come back with me and you are mine.' They started running and the ghost chased after them. Finally the ghost caught them, they fell down a hole with swirls going around and around.

Their mum and dad kept searching for them, but they couldn't find them. No one ever saw them again.

Catriona Quirke (8)
Our Lady Of Lourdes RC Primary School

JACK AND THE WOLF

Once upon a time there lived a boy called Jack. Jack was a shepherd with his dad and they owned a big field in the countryside. Every day Jack would have to take the sheep to the field to feed themselves. He would go in the morning and come back at night.

One day Jack was getting bored of his job so he decided to start shouting, 'Help the wolf's eaten my sheep!' Everyone came and when they came over they found him laughing. Jack did this for a few days, until one day the wolf really did come and eat some of his sheep and he bit Jack's leg. Jack was in hospital. Everyone came to see him and he said, 'Sorry for lying.'

Fam Samaan (9)
Our Lady Of Lourdes RC Primary School

DANGEROUS TRAINERS

One day there was a boy called Tom. Tom had a brother called Jack and a sister called Emma.

That day Tom's mum Sally needed to buy some shoes for Jack.
'I want blue and red shoes, no yellow and green,' said Jack.
'I'll get you whatever they have,' said Sally.

When they arrived at the shoe shop all the shoes were horrible. They went inside and there was the best pair of trainers ever with shiny red, blue, green and yellow on them.
'Wow,' said Jack. 'Buy them.'
'Are you sure?' said Sally.
'Yes.'
'OK,' said Sally.
They went back home and Tom tried them on, 'Wow!'

That night when Tom was still awake he saw the trainers move. 'Wow!' he said. Tom followed them and the trainers were eating all the food. 'Nooo!' said Tom. Tom picked them up and threw them in the garbage!

Luke Percival (8)
Our Lady Of Lourdes RC Primary School

THE GREEN GHOUL

Once there was an old, forbidden house. Nobody ever knew who lived in it. One dark night three boys were in the old house. It was very dark in there, so one of the boys got his torch out. They could see two glowing eyes. Out of the darkness came the most horrid face. He had a green face, green teeth and slime dripping out of his face.

He said, 'You're mine now.' At this they ran off and didn't look back. But the ghoul caught them and tripped them, then he went back to the house.

The next day they went back, it was not so scary or so they thought . . .

Nobody saw the ghoul again but he comes back every year and eats lots of people. Tell me if you see him, you never know, he might come to your door . . .

Lewis Sylvester (8)
Our Lady Of Lourdes RC Primary School

THE SCARY SLEEPOVER

A long time ago in a rusty house there lived an old witch who was making ghosts to put in people's living rooms.

One night a girl called Emily was so excited because the next night her friend Mollie was staying the night. The next day Mollie came over, she gave her mum a kiss and her mum went home.

The girls played games until soon it was bedtime, but they had a feast. They had biscuits and a chocolate egg. When Emily's mum was asleep and the sky was dark Emily and Mollie got scared because Mollie thought she saw something so they started to cry.

Then they forgot and fell asleep and in the living room they saw a ghost from the witch and they all ran. The girls investigated how the ghost got there. They said, 'We have to stop the ghosts!'

So off they went to the witch's house and chopped the witch up and the ghosts all faded. Then they had a party.

Emily Farrell
Our Lady Of Lourdes RC Primary School

THE MOVING STATUE

Once there was a moving statue. His name was Peter. People say that the statue can be a good sign or a bad sign. Some people even hate the statue so much they always hit him and sometimes they even run away from the statue.

Last time he went to the park, and when they saw him, they all looked at the statue and they did not realised that it was the statue because he was dressed up in some cool clothes, but the clothes were too big for him. The clothes all fell off him and he was back in his old, boring clothes. They all turned back and saw him in his boring clothes so they all ran and ran. The statue decided to go to a shopping centre.

Now the statue could not find a shopping centre but he found a supermarket, so he went in there. All the people stopped looking and turned because they could hear footsteps. When they saw the statue they all ran very, very fast, even the old ladies were running as fast as they could! Everyone ran out of the supermarket.

The statue kept on looking for something to buy but then he found a little boy but the statue just walked past. The statue could not find anything to buy so he walked out of the supermarket and saw a shopping centre. He went in the shopping centre and again everyone looked at him and the same thing happened. This time he bought a lot of things like cakes, toys, bikes, a car, food, ice cream, Coke and some lemonade. He paid for all of it and went.

He saw a lady statue standing outside waiting for him. He went outside and he fell in love, and lived happily ever after.

Jude D'Souza (8)
Our Lady Of Lourdes RC Primary School

MARIOS AND THE SECRET ROOM

One day there was a boy called Marios. He wore green trainers a blue T-shirt, black shoes and a red cap. He was funny, short and a good footballer.

He had two friends called Luke and Gian-Paolo, actually they were best friends. They liked playing football at play times, it was a good game to play. It was their favourite game.

Then Marios saw a little door and Gian-Paolo saw a bottle.
Marios said, 'Look, I've found a little door.'
Gian-Paolo said, 'Look I've found a medium-sized bottle.'

Then Luke, Marios and Gian-Paolo drank from the bottle and shrunk. They found a key and went through the door. A lot happened next but that's another story!

Luke Kelly (7)
Our Lady Of Lourdes RC Primary School

THE DRAGON IN THE PLAYGROUND

Once upon a time there were two children and they arrived at school early. Nobody was at school or in the playground, they were all alone.

Then one boy saw an egg, it was a very big egg. It had green, red, yellow and blue dots. It had one big different-coloured spiral right in the middle of the egg. It had nine different coloured stripes - one was blue, another was green, another was yellow, all sorts of colours that you can think of.
'What was that?' said the boy.
'It's the egg cracking,' said another boy and it was.
'Roar,' went the dragon.

The teacher came out to see what was happening and when she saw the dragon she went back into the school to phone the police. After that the teacher called the zoo too, so it could come and take the dragon away.

The dragon smashed the school down and ate all of the teachers, all of the food and all of the drink in the school. Then the police and the zoo came!

Then a big helicopter came holding a big net and it fired the big net at the dragon and because the net was as big as the dragon it almost caught it but the dragon dodged the net.

The dragon saw a burning building so it ran to the building. When it was there it did a gigantic sneeze and blew the fire from the building and the dragon was the hero!

Gian-Paolo Ferdenzi (7)
Our Lady Of Lourdes RC Primary School

THE DRAGON IN THE PLAYGROUND

One night a dragon snuck into the town and by the time he got there it was morning. He didn't notice it was morning, but he was in the school playground. When the dragon was sneaking about a child saw the dragon and passed the message on that there was a dragon about.

The person next to the teacher told him about the dragon, so the teacher went to all the classes and told the other teachers about the dragon. Then he rang the police and the firemen, but when they came the dragon was gone.

The next day the dragon went back to the school and he was doing the same thing as he'd done the day before, but it was a bit different. The police saw him, but the dragon did not see them. When the dragon did see them he blew fire at the policemen, but the dragon missed. The policemen shot at the dragon. The dragon blew his fire and one of the policemen died. Then everyone turned up.
Jude said, 'What's going on?'

When they saw the dead policeman the firemen went nearer to the dragon but he blew his fire out. Then a policeman shot the dragon in the leg and he died. The next day they buried the policeman.

Christopher Demetriou (8)
Our Lady Of Lourdes RC Primary School

THE BULLY

There was once a boy called Tom. He had to move as his dad had got a new job.

At his new school he got bullied by a boy called Ben. Ben said, 'I hate new kids, they get all the attention.' Tom got angry but he said nothing. In class Ben threw and flicked things at Tom's head. Tom got very angry, but he didn't do anything.

When he got back home from his new school his mum and dad said, 'How was your first day at school?'
Tom said, 'Fine.'
His mum said, 'You don't sound fine, what happened Tom?'
Tom said, 'I got bullied by Ben Gill.'
His mum said, 'Don't worry he will stop sooner or later.'
Tom said, 'Okay then.'

The next few days Ben did the same to Tom. After a week of bullying Tom was mad-crazy, he was so angry he wanted to be the bully.

Soon Ben was getting nicer but he didn't stop. Tom wanted to kill him, he was so, so angry at Ben he was going crazy.

At Ben's house he was playing darts with the school photos, he hit Tom's face over and over again. They were rivals.

At school Ben started to bully Tom again but it was too much for him, his eyes looked like red-hot coals, he punched Ben in the face and stomach. From that day on Ben was a nice boy!

Nnamdi Nwanokwu (8)
Our Lady Of Lourdes RC Primary School

THE ROYAL ROMANCE

There was once a prince called Federico, Prince of Spain who loved a girl called Lucy. They loved each other and wanted to be together forever, but there was only one problem, their families hated each other.

Prince Federico wouldn't let anyone stand in their way so every afternoon they would run off together into the woods.

This happened for months but one of the times the butler (Jeeves) heard the prince talking and told the king what Prince Federico and Lucy were doing. After the king heard this he decided to follow them. The king did this for quite some time and saw how in love they were so he decided they could marry each other even though he hated Lucy's family.

A week later they got married and had a really big and wonderful wedding. They also found out that Lucy (now Princess Minani) was pregnant and 9 months later she gave birth to a baby girl who was called Katherine which brought both families together, in fact they even liked each other. Both families had patched everything up and they all lived happily ever after.

Rosanna Marriott (11)
Our Lady Of Lourdes RC Primary School

MURDER IN THE NIGHT

Friday morning and still nothing, not even a call. While I was worrying about the business, the bimbo (Ray) who worked with me was sitting down reading. *Ring, ring.* I picked it up in excitement. A minute later we were in the car driving to a mansion in the countryside, someone had been murdered.

When we got there the maid came out and said, 'There's blood everywhere.' She looked really pale. We got inside and there was blood everywhere, so I got my magnifying glass and followed the trail of blood while Ray was interviewing the maid, cook and the butler. What I noticed was the blood was really light, I thought it could be ketchup so I licked it with my finger and it was.

By the time I had finished with the downstairs I looked upstairs and there were drops of blood leading from the bathroom to the bedroom and also a towel saturated in blood, this time it was blood. I slowly walked into the bedroom and a body was dumped in the wardrobe and on the table there were two glasses, one with bright pink lipstick on it and a cigarette.

I talked to Ray and he said it was the maid and so did I. We arrested the maid when she confessed and she said she'd done it because she wasn't getting paid a lot. She was jailed for life.

Matteo Mariani (9)
Our Lady Of Lourdes RC Primary School

A GOOD BOOK

As usual Joanna went for a browse round the local shopping centre. There was nothing worth spending money on. She must have been walking around for at least an hour and was getting bored.

Then in the bookshop window lay the greatest ever book, it was called *A Day In This Life*. She had to get it. She just had to. But as she imagined being the envy of her mates she heard a crack as the shop door opened and a crowd rushed in, she did the same.

In the shop it was close to a riot, people running, people shouting and books flying through the air and then the book landed in her hands. The only problem was it was also in the grip of Lisa, the school bully but she wasn't gonna bully Joanna out of this.

She pulled at the book, so did Joanna, then Lisa started crying for no reason. 'Oh stop the waterworks,' said Joanna but Lisa just kept on crying. Then the shopkeeper got involved and Lisa told him that Joanna had kicked her and sworn at her and of course the shopkeeper believed her.

In the end Joanna was banned from the bookshop for life and Lisa got the book which turned out to be rubbish and a teacher caught Lisa bullying!

Emma-Louise Amanshia (11)
Our Lady Of Lourdes RC Primary School

LOVE CHEAT

Queen Beatrice and her husband King William were deeply in love. They were together as one and they thought nothing would beat them. But there was one problem, their daughter, Miliano. To most people she was sweet and kind, including her parents, but little did they know she was dead set on splitting them up because she was jealous.

One day Princess Miliano told her mother that her father had ordered Beatrice to go and see him, but being stubborn, she sent him a note saying how annoyed she was.

Later on Miliano confessed to her father that she thought her mother was having an affair with Lord Ensigna as she had seen her sneaking out to meet him a lot. This fumed the King and he broke out in a rage. He then went to find Beatrice but she had disappeared.

When the Queen arrived home her husband accused her of his thoughts and she felt very upset and untrusted so she told him she was leaving which brought a smile to Miliano's face.

A few days later the King's maid persuaded William to get in contact with the Queen and they decided to meet.

When they got together they reminisced and questioned each other until they realised that Miliano had made it all up, so when they got home they asked her to leave and they never saw her again.

Gemma Sinnott (11)
Our Lady Of Lourdes RC Primary School

ROMANCE RUN AWAY

Once upon a time there was a queen, a king and their beautiful daughter, Princess Annabel. They all lived happily in their wonderful mansion just out of the city, near the countryside.

On Princess Annabel's 16th birthday they held a banquet and invited all the dukes, princes, kings and important handsome young men from all over the country for their daughter to marry.

Princess Annabel was not very happy about this as she had been secretly dating the handsome peasant boy whom she had met at market and was planning to run away with him the following week, but time had been cut short as her father wanted her to pick someone to marry by the following day. Princess Annabel was distraught at this and decided to tell her true love William that night so she set off to see him.

William was a well-mannered, gentle man who happened to be very poor as his father had died.
'William,' whispered Princess Annabel.
'Yes,' replied William who had appeared out of nowhere.
'Oh William, you will never guess what has just happened . . . Well Father wants me to marry and oh can we run away tonight? I have packed all my possessions,' Princess Annabel said as she burst into tears.
'Do not cry my dear we will leave straight away. I will pack my things and then we'll leave for the city,' William answered sensibly.

As soon as William had packed they walked to William's carriage and left for the city but little did they know what was to await them . . .

Camilla Iesini (10)
Our Lady Of Lourdes RC Primary School

THE GHOST OF GUY FAWKES

The ghost of Guy Fawkes! Well this is the story of how me and my mate, Matt, got really scared when we saw it . . . the ghost of Guy Fawkes!

Two years, four days, eleven hours and twenty-seven minutes ago me and Matt were chasing some absolutely gorgeous girls into the forest when . . . we saw it. Out of the leaves and trees we saw it . . . the ghost of Guy Fawkes!

We ran and ran and ran as fast as we could but it was right behind us. We ran nearly four miles but it was still right behind us.

Ten minutes later we walked away and that is the scariest thing that has happened to me and my mate. Neither of us have ever been in a forest since and we don't like Bonfire Night anymore either!

Jake Hennessey (11)
Our Lady Of Lourdes RC Primary School

ETERNAL XIII

Steve. A name you might enjoy or despise during the course of this story. Before I go on I should tell you about Steve, he is a short (4ft 7in to be precise) European, 13-year-old boy who goes to Middleton Secondary School. While I am writing about this dreadful tale, Steve, his very stupid friend, Luke and Steve's mum and dad were being whisked away to Dover to begin their 4-star Atlantic cruise that Steve's mother, Hyacinth had won 3 months previously.

As Steve looked and watched with great anticipation at the magnificently crafted cruise ship, his parents and friend boarded. 'Quick everyone is boarding, come now!' Steve took as long as he could.

The next morning Steve felt strange; strangely strange. 'Luke,' he asked, 'do you feel strange?' Luke snored away. Steve got changed and went to brush his teeth but he got side-tracked and ended up on the deck. As he turned back he saw a ghostly white man. Steve screamed and legged it back on to the deck towards the captain's quarters. He kicked the door open and ran in. 'Captain . . .' he panted as he told the chair what happened.

Steve glanced to see a gun. 'Captain,' he enquired as the chair swivelled around . . . to find an empty chair. Steve picked up the gun and waved it around threateningly. He ran back down to his cabin to find the man had not moved an inch. 'I've got a gun,' said Steve weakly as the cardboard cut out fell down and one side of the ship until there was no ship left apart from the deck.

Steve screamed and cried even though no one could hear him. 'Too bad,' shouted a voice, 'maybe next time.' As the words *Eternal XIII* appeared in blood on the pieces of wood stranded in the ocean.

Jack McCormack-Noonan (11)
Our Lady Of Lourdes RC Primary School

THE DIARY OF MADALIN GOOSENBERRY

17/5/07

Dear Diary,

Why me? What have I done? I'm such a geek! I have no popular friends. I'm such a misfit. I'm not in with the fashion, I wear glasses 10 times too big, I'm hairy, spotty, but worst of all I have to wear a head brace 24/7. I'm so ugly. None of the popular boys fancy me. My mum said it's just a teenage phase I have to go through. There's this really popular boy that I like and when I asked him out he rejected me. What am I complaining about? I have a boyfriend! Well maybe I should be complaining, all he is is a male version of me. He is so ugly that we have to have a secret relationship. No one must find out!

18/5/07

Dear Diary,

Oh my goodness! 1) Me and Edward were kissing in secret and Jason (the one I like) saw us. The worst part is our head braces got stuck so Jason had to untangle us. How embarrassing. 2) An anonymous person wrote a letter to me saying they were going to tell the whole school what happened. This is like an episode of EastEnders. What am I going to do?

Catherine Rooney (11)
Our Lady Of Lourdes RC Primary School

THE BLOODY STORY

One evening in a house in the country, (not just any old house, it was the murder house) there was a butler, a maid and a cook. They were the Thompson family's staff - the family were a woman named Detty, a man named Tom, a boy named Junior and a little girl named Lucy.

One evening the cook was in the kitchen which was outside of the house. Where they lived, of course, was by a warm beach in Spain, anyway back to the story, as I was saying - the cook heard a noise outside but little did he know that when he went out to look about another person came in. He decided to go back in and start cooking, then *bang, bang, bang.* The cook had been shot dead on the floor.

The Thompson's decided to go and look in the kitchen to see what was taking the cook so long, then they saw him with all blood splattered on the floor. They called the police who interviewed the maid. Firstly they asked, 'Where were you at the time of the crime?'
She replied, 'Doing housework like I usually do.'

As the clock struck twelve midnight the Thompson's were scared stiff thinking to themselves, *there's a murderer in our house.*

The next day a sword was put right through the butler onto the wall. It left a note, 'Leave this house and I won't kill'.

They found out that it was the maid because of all the blood on her hands, so they left the house and gave the keys to the crazy maid then burnt down the house and the maid burnt to death.

The family left the house and lived in a cottage near a road so if a murderer came into their house they would be able to get away quickly and they lived frightfully ever after.

Tommaso Serena   (11)
Our Lady Of Lourdes RC Primary School

THE DIARY OF KYLIE NOCH

21.4.98

Dear Diary,

Today I had to say goodbye to my true love, Tommy. He is in the navy and it was so sad to see him get shipped away. He was crushed, literally crushed. You see when they throw the anchors out it makes the boat still. Well, when it happened, let's just say he didn't end up in hospital for nothing. Yes, that's right, the anchor fell on him. Now here I am, two weeks later, he's dead. I don't know how I'm going to cope.

22.4.98

Dear Diary,

Today I saw the cutest boy ever. Now, I know that my boyfriend has just died but it's time to move on. Anyway he asked me out and I said yes. But, he reminds me of someone, someone like Tommy. Maybe Tommy's spirit went into Kyle's body. Wow! This is amazing. I never thought that Tommy would come back. Now that he has we can get married and have lots of kids and live in a cosy cottage. Yeah!

Emma Inzani (11)
Our Lady Of Lourdes RC Primary School

Lily

Once upon a time in a faraway land there lived a king, queen and a princess. They all lived together in a castle. The princess had long, golden hair that shone in the sun like a primrose on a bright summer's morning shining for all to see, skin that was as white as blossom falling from the trees and beautiful eyes that were as green as emeralds. She was always smiling, however there was one problem.

The king and queen wanted Lily (the princess) to marry a prince called James but she didn't want to marry James, she wanted to wait for the right man. She did not love James. One day Lily went out for a walk and saw a poor widower. The widower said, 'Find the one who you love in your heart and everything will work out for you.'

That night Lily dreamt she met a man who she loved very much and she married him and they lived happily ever after. She woke up with a smile thinking, *dreams can come true,* and went back to bed.

When she woke up she had a bath and got dressed. She wore a beautiful dress and went out to find that someone.
The king shouted at the top of his voice, 'Where are you going, to find someone?'
'How did you know?' replied Lily.
'Finally seen sense, going to see James,' he said in a low voice.
'No, well you could say that,' she smiled and with these words she ran off.

Eventually she came to a bridge, crossed over and on the other side she met a gorgeous, handsome man. 'Hello,' said Lily shyly.
'Hello, what's your name?' he called.
'Lily and yours?'
'Mark, maybe we can go out?' he said.
'I'd love to!' she shouted.

Two months later Lily and Mark got married. A month before James had died. Lily loved Mark more than anything in the world. Her dream had come true and she was happy and so were the king and queen.

Deborah Wharton (11)
Our Lady Of Lourdes RC Primary School

A TWISTED LOVE!

'Darling, what would you like for your tea?' asked Mrs Catherine Sheberg, a very rich and powerful lady, to her husband Mr Bert Sheberg, twice as old and twice as powerful.

Mrs Sheberg walked into the swimming pool room. 'Aarrgghh!' screamed Mrs Sheberg dropping the tray of caviar (Mr Sheberg's favourite dish). Mr Sheberg was lying, face down with a knife through his back in the swimming pool! 'Bert!' gasped Catherine, hand to her mouth.

Catherine ran to the nearest phone and rang the police, they said they would call detectives and they would be there as soon as possible. Mrs Sheberg put down the phone, looked at Mr Sheberg, then carried on with her daily routine, washing Mr Sheberg's clothes but she wouldn't have to wash much longer, with Bert . . . well gone!

Ding-dong! Went the door bell outside Mrs Sheberg's mansion. A pale, skinny figure answered the door. 'Oh, hello, you must be the detectives,' said Catherine shaking the two detectives hands. They all entered the giant sitting room.

'Mrs Sheberg, I know this must be a very inconvenient time with your husband's death, but we would like to ask you a few questions,' said a detective called Jenny Spanna.
'Are you accusing me of murdering my husband?' exclaimed Catherine standing up with a shocked but extremely surprised tone in her voice.
'No, no, Ma'am, it's procedure, please don't be offended!' said the other detective, Clifford Travis.
'I'm not offended, I'm disgusted! Me, that's appalling,' said Mrs Sheberg looking very twitchy. 'Fine, then, ask away!' she said sipping her fifth glass of wine.

The detectives asked questions, but still, they suspected she wasn't telling the whole story. The detectives found out a lot about Mrs Sheberg, she was an alcoholic and had a bit of trouble with her anger, she had taken drugs (she said she thought it was an aspirin) and she'd accidentally cut herself with a knife when she was cutting a carrot. The detectives definitely thought she was the killer!

Detective Spanna looked around the house, questioned the neighbours, the maid, butler and chauffeur. But still they had a feeling that Mrs Catherine Sheberg was not the innocent housewife she seemed to be!

Mrs Parkinson looked out the kitchen window, she could see the butler shouting at Mrs Sheberg, she was crying, she got on her knees, it looked like she was pleading for dear life! Mrs Parkinson was the Sheberg's neighbour, and she phoned the police, who got hold of the restless detectives, she told them everything she had seen! Could Mrs Sheberg and the butler be in the murder together or was it an affair between them? The detectives were extremely puzzled, maybe it wasn't Mrs Sheberg after all! Maybe Catherine was asking why he did it, maybe the butler was jealous of the two lovebirds and maybe, just maybe the butler was the killer! There was so many maybes!

The next week for the detectives was hard, everywhere Catherine and the butler went the detectives would follow! To the detectives it felt like a game of hide-and-seek, to the other two they were completely unaware the detectives were on to the butler.

Another week passed, the detectives had evidence about the butler killing Mr Sheberg, they had got a recorded conversation and fingerprints from the knife matching the butler's. The detectives would have thought that the butler would have been smarter, to wear gloves, that didn't have a hole in them!

The detectives found their killer and they were pretty proud! As for the butler he won't be serving people at home for a very long time!

Megan Fellows (11)
Our Lady Of Lourdes RC Primary School

THE DEMON OF THE HILLTOP

Hi, my name's Charlie (short for Charlotte) and I'm going to tell you what happened to me and my friend Stell when we went for a short walk. Guess what happened in the end? Well you'll have to read on and find out.

Well, as I told you, me and my friend, Stell, went on a walk and as we went we noticed a hill just outside of our town. What made it even more freaky was that it had a mansion on top! We decided to explore. That was a very wrong decision.

As we got to the top of the hill we kicked the door open and echoes filled the house. 'Come on, let's go it's too eerie for me,' Stell whispered. Just then a greeny-brown, scaly animal jumped out across the room. 'Heeloo,' the animal said, 'come to seeee meee?'
'Aarrgghh!' we yelled together.

The animal pushed us in, took hold of Stell and took her in a room. I saw a bright flash of light. They both came back but instead of the brown-haired, brown-eyed Stell there came an ugly brown animal. 'Take her down!' she cried . . .

I ran until I lost them and from that day on no one ever saw Stell again. And that was the end of her or was it?

Ruby Lowe (11)
Our Lady Of Lourdes RC Primary School

WHERE'S MUM?

'Mum, what's for dinner?' shouted Becky, but there was no answer.
'Mum?' Becky shouted again as she was walking upstairs.
'Oh erm, roast chicken darling,' replied Mum.
Then Becky switched on the TV and watched a programme about mystery and crime. 'I wish I could be a detective,' wailed Becky.

Suddenly a loud scream came from upstairs. Becky thought that this could be a good opportunity for her, so she sneaked upstairs and went to her mum's bedroom but she wasn't there. Becky searched around but there was no sign of her mum. She rang her mum's mobile but there was no answer.

This isn't a game anymore, she thought. Then she called the police. They said they were going to try to find her mum. Becky sat down and started to bite her nails.

About an hour later they rang to tell Becky that they'd found her mum and they had arrested the criminals.
'Thank you so much,' cried Becky with relief.

When her mum came home she made a cup of tea and then Becky's mum fell asleep.

Julia Buschi (9)
Our Lady Of Lourdes RC Primary School

THE LOST DOG

I went into the kitchen. Mum and Dad were checking if everything was OK as that afternoon we were going to Ireland to stay with Granny and Grandad.

It was time to go. It was 2.30, so we ordered a taxi. It took an hour to get there and our flight was at 4.50. We checked in and had a look around.

An hour later a lady said, 'Please go to your gates.'
It was 4.30. Time passed and then it was time to go. We boarded the plane. During the journey I read a book and an hour later we arrived. Grandad was there to pick us up.

When we arrived at Granny and Grandad's house, Granny came and gave me a big kiss. I wanted to go and see my cousin Bridget. She had a dog and her name was Ginger.
'Shall we take a walk?' asked Bridget.
'OK,' I replied.
We went up the street chatting. Suddenly, we noticed Ginger had gone. She must have run off. *'Ginger!'* we called. We searched for ages but then we gave up and went home. There she was!
'We were looking for you, Ginger!' I said.
'She came home just a few minutes ago,' said Granny.
Thank goodness she was alright! Next time I'll keep a good eye on her.

Julia Kenny (9)
Our Lady Of Lourdes RC Primary School

CLARA'S BIRTHDAY

One day I woke up and was lying in bed for fifteen minutes or so. I knew, I just knew there was something special I had to do. I suddenly sat up and said, 'Clara's birthday!' I got up, washed and then got dressed.

Downstairs, I remembered I had to help my mum and dad to prepare for my older sister's twelfth birthday.

As time passed, Clara woke up and all her friends were there. I got her a frog and she called it Froggy. She had always liked frogs. Clara's friends were called Emily, Julia, Susan, Catriona and Cinzia. We had a great time!

Isabella Bonato (9)
Our Lady Of Lourdes RC Primary School

THE ABANDONED DEVIL HOUSE

There was once a house, no ordinary house, a cursed house! People called it this because of the day that Jack and Laura went into the house and never returned.

It was a summer's day and Jack and Laura were in a bad mood. They decided to invite their friends over to play a dare game. They sat in a circle and the first dare went to Laura and Jack. They had to go into the house.

They walked up to the house, opened the door and with trembling legs, they shuffled in. There was a staircase that led up a short distance. Cobwebs hung like silk. They started up the stairs and then they heard something. Then they felt something pass through them. Laura fainted. Somehow, something wasn't right. Jack held Laura up and he moved into a room. This room was chilly and dark and in a far corner was a coffin. It was made out of wood with ancient writing on the top and was bolted down with gold locks.

Jack read out the words in the way he thought they were pronounced:- *'Actu misul dico neo.'* Translated, this was, 'Ancient vampires arise for I bring you a sacrifice.'

The coffin bolts fell to the ground and the coffin broke open revealing a monster's face with fangs. It grabbed Laura. Jack heard a noise and more vampires came.

Jack found an axe but it was too late, she was possessed by Satan. Her eyes were white and then she grew fangs, so Jack killed her before she could kill. He took another swing and missed. He heard a voice say, 'Barlow, get him!' He swung again and killed them all in a row, but one in the basement survived.

Jack got trapped in the house and died of old age. Some say that Jack killed the monster in the basement, but I say the vampire is still skulking around looking for Jack's body.

Dino Raucci (9)
Our Lady Of Lourdes RC Primary School

THE WHATSIT BOY!

There once was a boy named Barry who had strange and magical powers. He was able to transform himself into anything or anybody just by saying, 'Whatsit, whatsit' and adding the name of the person or object he wanted to change into.
He had two brothers and a sister called Larry, Harry and Sally.

Barry had a huge test that he hadn't studied for. He had to do something quickly, so he said 'Whatsit, whatsit, Mr Rubberneck!'
It's important for you to know that Mr Rubberneck was the headmaster.

At ten past nine he said to Mrs Wojewodzki, 'Don't you know it is a holiday?'
'No,' said Mrs Wojewodzki.
'Well then, class dismissed!' said Barry.

A few minutes later the real Mr Rubberneck said, 'What are you doing?'
'You said it was a holiday,' replied Mrs Wojewodzki.
'No I didn't!' exclaimed Mr Rubberneck.
'Then who did?' said Mrs Wojewodzki.

It was lucky for Barry and the rest of the class that the two puzzled teachers never did find out what happened that day and the rumour was that the two teachers spent the rest of the day drinking tea. Barry, meanwhile, went home to play with Larry, Harry and Sally.

James Landi (10)
Our Lady Of Lourdes RC Primary School

REVENGE

This is a story of 3 against 3.

There was an abandoned church on an icy cliff with a graveyard below the length of a swimming pool. This was the hang-out place of three bad guys known as Rocky (the nasty bully), Sneaky (cos he tells lies) and the leader, Tricky (the thief of the gang who, if there's something to steal, he will steal it). This gang is called Hurricane.

One day, just as Hurricane were leaving the scene of a bank robbery they had carried out, they bumped into the three goodies, otherwise known as Michael, Luke and Bruce. Tricky shouted, 'Leg it!' and they ran away, followed by the good guys who kept well out of sight.

Rocky, Sneaky and Tricky all met back at their base to count their stolen money which meant that the good guys now knew where they were hiding. They hatched a plan to make them return the goods and hand themselves in. This plan involved dressing up.

They went home and changed into their Hallowe'en costumes. They met back at the church to carry out the rest of their plan.

They snuck into the hide-out dressed as a vampire, zombie and skeleton shouting, 'Give the money back, hand yourselves in,' over and over again.
They scared the living daylights out of Hurricane who screamed and begged for mercy, saying, 'S-s-sorry we stole the money, we promise not to do it ever again. P-p-please don't hurt us.'
The goodies told them to go to the police and tell them everything.

When they got there with the stolen goods, the police didn't believe their story about being spooked, but because of the money they got put behind bars for a very long time.

The goodies were pleased with themselves and all agreed that it's better to be a goodie than a baddie!

Joe Donaghy (10)
Our Lady Of Lourdes RC Primary School

BUSTED AND ME

One sunny afternoon when I was on my holidays in Spain, I went for a short walk. As I was walking along, I spotted a ticket on the floor. I bent down and to my surprise it was a ticket to go and see Busted on tour.

I quickly hurried along to the shop to get the sweets and some bread for my family. After leaving the shop I ran all the way back to the apartment and told the rest of my family what I had found, but they didn't believe me and began to laugh. I was so excited that I was nearly crying with happiness. In my mind I kept on saying, *I'm going to see Busted live* and I was jumping up and down and playing my CD of them out loud.

The next day was the day of the concert, so I woke up early, had my breakfast and got washed. I ran to get dressed into my Busted T-shirt and shorts. Then I ran into the other room to see if my mum had finished doing my banner to take with me.

My dad dropped me off at the concert where loads of people were waiting to get in. When the concert started, it was wicked because my favourite member of the band was at the front of the stage. My favourite member is Matt. He is wicked the way that he jumps so high and still plays the guitar. The band played my favourite songs - 'Year 3000' and 'You Said No'.

After the concert I went to the stage door where I got my T-shirt signed. My dad came to collect me and when I got back to the apartment I said that maybe next time they will believe me when I say that I have found something. They all said that they would and said sorry to me.

The rest of my holiday soon passed by, but I couldn't wait to get back home and tell all my friends.

Laura Dyer (9)
Our Lady Of Lourdes RC Primary School

THREE DAYS IN MY LIFE

One day I went to a mansion house on Broadwalk Road. I think this house was the biggest one I had seen in my life. My dad and I agreed that the garden was very big. My three friends said the same. We went and played football, 'it' and 'bulldog' and then stayed the night. I slept in with my dad and my friends slept in the spare room.

In the morning we went home. We had had a great time at the mansion house and it had been very hot. That morning was the 12th of August - one day away from my birthday and that night I thought that I was going to have a great day.

On my birthday I got my first phone, PlayStation 2 games, a memory card for my PS2 and a Nike shirt. I had a great party at the mansion.

Thomas Bunton (9)
Our Lady Of Lourdes RC Primary School

THE MYSTERY OF THE WOODS

One dark night, me and Shannen were walking the dog. It was dark in the woods and I could hear the owls hooting. We took a shortcut through the grass, but it was a wrong shortcut and we were lost! We kept on walking to see where we would end up.

About half an hour later we ended up in a farmyard. We saw an old, battered cottage and decided to go and ask if we could get directions. We knocked on the door . . . no reply. *Knock, knock* . . . no reply. We tried to knock again, but we couldn't because the door swung open and a wind pulled us in (even the dog).
'*Wow!* What was that?' Shannen said.
'I don't know,' I whispered.
We were both in a state of shock.
We started to walk slowly into a bedroom. We stood there and 1, 2, 3 . . . *pop!* A mummy popped out of a bed. We ran out into the front room and about 100 spiders ran out of the sofa. Next the kitchen and worse still, a hand came out of the sink! We ran out of the house. Oh my God, we were home! *Wow!*

'Where were you?' screamed Mum.
'Well me and Shannen went on an adventure,' I said.
'An adventure! You were meant to be at school three hours ago!' Mum said.
'I'm sorry, Mum, but we were walking the dog and well . . . we got lost,' I said crying.
'Ahh, don't cry. Come here, I forgive you.'

Gemma Murray (9)
Our Lady Of Lourdes RC Primary School

A SAD GIRL

Once there was a girl called Amy. She went on holiday to Spain with her friends Nicole, Joe and Thomas.

When they got there, Amy remembered that her parents didn't know that she was going to Spain so she was worried. She couldn't tell her friends because they would be angry.

Later on that day they went looking for a place to live. Suddenly, Amy heard Thomas, Joe and Nicole scream. Amy looked to the right and left and around the corner of the street.

The next day Amy went to the police station and told them what had happened. After that she went searching, but she couldn't find them and didn't know what to do.

Eventually, she went back home. When she got there, she heard the bang of the door. She was so afraid that someone might kill her, but suddenly the telephone rang. She didn't want to answer it, but then the door went bang again, but no one was there. Amy heard some laughing at the back of the door. When she looked it was Nicole, Joe and Thomas. They were playing a trick on her.

The next day they went back to London. Amy's parents were not angry and the four of them had just had so much fun.

Nicole Panisales (10)
Our Lady Of Lourdes RC Primary School

UNTITLED

One morning my friend and I were on a coach trip with the school. Everyone was excited because we were going to a house on top of the mountain. My friend, Giusy, was nervous and asked if there were any ghosts, vampires or mummies. I told her that there were no such things as ghosts, vampires or even mummies.

When we got there, a bent man with a walking stick welcomed us. He talked in a low voice like a fated man waiting to blow up. When we entered the house we heard people screaming from upstairs. The man said we could look around and our teacher told us to stay with our partners.

Me and Giusy walked down the hallway which had iron men with swords in their hands. As we walked two men facing each other dropped their swords and nearly hit us. After that we ran to the teacher but she didn't believe us and neither did the police, so we went home. After a few minutes a letter arrived in the post. It was for me and said that I needed to meet this person in the park alone.
When I went to school I told Giusy about it and she'd got one too.

We went together to the park and found the person. I asked him his name and he replied, 'Don't ask.'
Giusy said, 'Should we be talking to strangers?'
I replied, 'No,'
'So why are we talking to this one?' she said.
'Because he knows something about something,' I said.
The stranger said he was a detective and he found clues of what happened and who had done it. He said it was the keeper of the house and he killed people and turned them into statues.

Chrystel Keegan (10)
Our Lady Of Lourdes RC Primary School

THE ADVENTURES OF YEAR 5

It was a good day for me, it was my birthday. Everyone was saying 'happy birthday' to me.

Everybody thought we were a strong class so they called us the army class. Then we got a letter on the computer. It was from the president. He said we had to swim across the river and kill the robots. So me and Year 5 went to cross the river. Everybody got across except Mina, Oraph and Conor.

Then their were two ways - over or under. Half of the class went over and the other half went under. I went under, the ones that went over got blown up by some bombs and got wrapped up by mummies. The ones that went under had to fight vampires. We killed them all.

There were fourteen of us left in the class. Soon it was night. We stayed in a hotel for one night then the next day we went to the gun shop to buy big guns. It took us five days to get to the robots.

It was the 22nd of June and a big machine was controlling the robots. The leader of the robots was Goldberg. We tried stabbing Goldberg and his friends, but they would not die, so we tried shooting them. All that did was knock them on the floor. When we ran over them, they just got back up.

It became night so we went back to the hotel to go to bed. I had a dream about how to build them. My brain said to shoot the machine and shoot the robots in their eyes.

It was morning. I went into the lab and I shot the machines and I shot the robots in their eyes. I took the electric chips out of their heads and put them in the bin. Then the president said he was going to make good robots to help people.

There were five children left; me, Mikey, Joe, James and Chrystel. We went home to tell our mums all about it.

Shane McDonald (10)
Our Lady Of Lourdes RC Primary School

THE KILLER

One day in my office I got a call. There was a man on the phone. It was a private detective, Joe.

He said, 'Come to the graveyard, I'm being held hostage.'

I went to the office next door to me. It had another detective named Connor. I told him what had happened and I said, 'Let's grab two pairs of wheels.'

When we got to the graveyard, we couldn't see anyone so we walked around a bit and still couldn't see anyone. Connor leaned against a wall and then a trapdoor opened. We both fell in. Then we saw Joe. He was tied up on a chair and he was gagged. As soon as we saw Joe, we went to untie his hands, but he jumped up and I saw his hands were free, not tied at all. In one hand he had a gun and was pointing it at me.

'You killed my sister,' he shouted, 'and now I'm gonna kill you.'

'Your sister's death was an accident,' I replied. 'She was cleaning my gun when it went off. Anyway, the jury knew I was innocent.'

To my left I heard Connor click his revolver. 'What you didn't know was Joe's sister was my girlfriend and you're gonna die cleaning my gun.'

'Connor!' I gasped, 'You're my pal. You're my business partner!'

'We're gonna show you her grave and kill you there,' Connor shouted.

'OK, OK, but let the condemned man have a last drink, eh?' I said.

Within three minutes, Connor had brought my whisky bottle from the car, along with some plastic cups I keep in the boot. The three of us sat down and slowly we each sipped at the whisky. I kept pleading with them to spare my life, until I noticed Joe rock unsteadily on his chair. Then Connor dropped his plastic cup and his hand went limp.

Joe croaked, 'What . . . what have you done to us?'

'Just given you a dead man's drink. The powder I added to your whisky will take full effect in another minute,' I said.

'But . . . why . . .?' he trailed off.

'Why? Because I'm the killer,' I said.

Michael Hogan (9)
Our Lady Of Lourdes RC Primary School

UNTITLED

One day in a forest, a very long time ago, lived a king, queen and princess. The princess had never been to town before, so one morning she got her mother, the queen, to take her.

She saw a bakery - she liked cakes! She saw everything, lots she'd never seen before. She also saw a very handsome young man and then asked her mum, 'Mum, when can I meet a prince and get married?'
'Well,' said her mother, 'you can get married whenever you meet a prince you like.'
'Oh that's great because I have just seen someone I like,' answered the princess.
'Well, maybe you can come back and see him,' replied her mum.
'That will be great.'
Then they were on their way home.

When they got home the cook had made and served their dinner. They loved dinner time because they were always starving after they had been out. The princess had finished all her dinner and then had chocolate sponge for pudding. The princess was a very beautiful young lady with long, blonde hair. She had bright blue eyes, red, rosy lips, her skin was as white as snow and she had clean, white teeth.

Princess Mia had got every colour dress you could imagine and matching shoes to go with every dress. Mia looked a lot like her mum but her mum had brown hair instead of blonde and it was short not long. She had tanned skin instead of white, snowy skin. The king was totally different to the girls because he had got a beard, very short brown hair, pinky-peach lips, tanned skin, dull blue eyes and loads and loads of long red cloak with fluff on the edges.

The next day Princess Mia went to pick some berries in the forest. It was her sixteenth birthday and her parents had arranged a surprise birthday party. Everyone was invited, even the people from the town, including the boy that she liked. This was her chance to see if he liked her. She was dancing with another boy to make him jealous. Well, in the end he couldn't take it anymore. He had to go and ask her to dance with him.
'Will you dance with me?' asked the boy.

'Why yes, I will dance with you,' replied Mia. 'My name is Mia and it is my birthday today.'

'Well happy birthday and my name is William,' answered the boy.

Will was crying with happiness. He was so happy that he asked Mia to marry him. Mia had to go and ask her parents if she could marry him. Her mum said yes and so did her dad.

She went back to William and said, 'Yes, I will marry you. Come on and meet my parents, the king and queen.'

Mia's dad was called Stepon and her mum was called Elile.

'Mum, Dad, this is William and William this is my mum and dad, Stepon and Elile. Guess what? He has asked me to marry him and I have said yes. Mum, we would like to get married as soon as possible.'

'Well OK then,' said her parents excitedly.

A week later they were in a church getting married. When the church ceremony was finished, they went to their new home by the seaside.

Josephine Hennessey (10)
Our Lady Of Lourdes RC Primary School

AMY'S CHANCE

I was lying in bed. I was awake, but I didn't want to get up. I was trembling and had butterflies in my stomach. My bedroom door opened, but I ignored it. Just then my mum opened the curtains. The light came flooding through my window.

'Come on, get up,' shouted Mum. 'It's the final of the netball tournament.'

I didn't want to go, but I couldn't let my team down.

'You've only got two hours to get changed and get there, so hurry up!'

My mum nags a lot! It's really annoying.

Finally, I got up, had my breakfast and got changed. I rang my friend, Shannen, because she was playing in the match too.

'Hi, Shannen. I'm so nervous!' I exclaimed.

'I'm not,' she replied, 'just think about winning.'

'That might be a good idea, Shannen, thanks.'

'Bye Amy.'

Shannen's really kind.

'Come on Amy, get in the car,' Mum said.

I got in shaking.

When we got to the court, I saw Nicole and Chrystel drinking some water. They waved to me, so I ran over to them while my mum went to see my netball teachers, Emma and Jo. I wasn't so nervous now I was with my friends, but I knew when I walked onto the pitch I would get jelly legs. Just then Gemma, Josie and Shannen arrived. I realised Nicole and Chrystel had their bibs on, so I went to get mine. Joe had a basket of bibs, so I went over to her. I was hoping not to be anything important. Emma got her list and I was a . . . substitute! *Yes! Yes! Yes!* I would only be playing if someone was really hurt. *Yes!*

'Everyone on the pitch, please,' Jo yelled.

Everyone got in their positions very slowly. The opposite team began. They were like giraffes compared to our team.

There were two parts of the match. Each half was twenty minutes. Then minutes passed and it was 0-0. Each team had a chance, but they both missed. Seventeen minutes passed and still no goals. The other team were brilliant defenders, but my team were excellent attackers.

Half-time and the score was still 0-0. Everyone had a drink and a biscuit. Five minutes was up and the players went back on the pitch. We started this time and it was the same all through the second half as the first half.

Suddenly, in the sixteenth minute, Gemma, our goal shooter, fell over and her knee started bleeding. Emma got up, helped Gemma up and put me in her place. Our team got a free shoot. I had to take it. I had jelly legs. I stood frozen to the spot. I jumped up . . . *yes!* I scored. *Yes! Yes! Yes!* The whistle went for full-time. We had won! My friends carried me on their shoulders. We had won! *Yes!* I shook hands with the goalkeeper. I felt so happy. This was the best match I've ever played.

Amy Landi (10)
Our Lady Of Lourdes RC Primary School

THE GHOST COTTAGE

There was once a small cottage in a dark forest. There were three ghosts living in the cottage. They were named Butler Bob, Maid Mary and Crystel the cook. They had built the cottage whilst they were still alive, because they were trying to hide from an old friend, who turned out to be a witch. She had been trying to kill them so they built the cottage in the forest and lived there safely for a while. But the witch eventually found them and killed them.

That happened over 200 years ago and so now they live alone as ghosts in the cottage. In the front room there is a big grandfather clock. Whenever the clock strikes midnight, the three ghosts appear. They do not come out during the day because the cottage is now used as a museum. This was because detectives found the three dead bodies in the cottage and people came to look at the house because they wanted to see where the murder happened. People started to say that it was a witch that killed the three people, so it is now a Hallowe'en museum.

One night when the three ghosts were flying around the forest near their cottage, they met the witch who killed them. She shrieked, 'I thought you were dead!'
Crystel replied, 'We are *dead*, we are now *ghosts!*'
'Yes, no thanks to you,' said Butler Bob.
'I am so sorry that I killed you,' said the witch.
'Well it is too late for that. We have been ghosts for over 200 years, so it is very late to say you are sorry,' replied Mary. Suddenly, Mary realised that it would soon be daylight, so the ghosts had to get back to the cottage. 'Hurry,' she told the others.

But suddenly the witch shouted in a wicked voice, 'Where do you think you are going? You will not be around much longer.' She fired a bolt of fire at the ghosts but nothing happened. The ghosts flew away as fast as they could and finally got back to their cottage. When they looked at the grandfather clock, it was 6.01. Suddenly the cottage door was pushed open and there was the witch. They were scared that she would hurt them, but she looked around and said, 'Oh no, they got away from me.' She looked all over the house, but she could not see them. She waited for a while, but then she decided they weren't there so she decided not to bother them again.

Butler Bob, Maid Mary and Crystel the cook realised that as the witch had not seen them, neither could anybody else, so now they were free to be out in their cottage any time they liked. They would not be ghosts who only came out at night, but they could now play in their cottage day or night.

Guisy Ferracane (10)
Our Lady Of Lourdes RC Primary School

THE MANSION OF THE MURDERER'S CORPSE

The year is 1985. The two best agents the police have got (their names are Jones and Stacy) have a mission. They have to rid the mansion at the top of the hill of the swarming zombies. These zombies can only be killed by taking the murderer's corpse to the gallows (the place where you hang somebody).

Their boss, Sergeant Sebastian, codenamed 'Mr Big' said, 'We are in a crisis! The zombies came from the mansion and took the weapons away! We tried to hold them back but I only just survived!'

So after several minutes packing bullets and putting on armour, they went on their mission to the top of the hill.

On arrival at the mansion they found nothing until they entered it. There were about 10 zombies at the entrance and once they had killed them all, more came. When they went into the next room, a rotting zombie fired a rocket launcher shell at them. Jones nearly got hit! Then after they dealt with him, they finally found the corpse but it was moving! They shot a few blows to the head before it dropped down and died. When they picked up the corpse, so many enemies came that Stacy died. When they had been disposed of he took a few quiet minutes to pray as he and she were married.

When he returned the body of the murderer to the gallows he had saved the world.

Konrad Sterlini (10)
Our Lady Of Lourdes RC Primary School

WELCOME TO THE HAUNTED HOTEL

We were walking to a hotel from the seaside. Charlie, Justin Timberlake and I. There we saw it. Right in front of us we saw a posh hotel. It looked empty. I did the honours and rang the bell. We heard a voice, it bellowed, 'Come in.' We went in.

Charlie switched on the lights which were so bright, we thought we were blinded. Justin led us down the hallway. Charlie and I looked at peculiar pictures and we noticed they had moving eyes. We got out our notebooks and made a note of this.
By the time we had reached the end of the hallway, we met an ugly-looking zombie who showed us to our room. Justin was so lucky because he didn't have to share a room with anyone.

That evening when we had settled in, we went downstairs to eat. That's where we met the man in charge of the hotel. His name was Dracul and his assistant was Zobby. They were asking peculiar questions.
After our meal of raw meat and frozen chips, I went upstairs to use the loo. I saw white things going through the wall. They were ghosts. I went through the wrong room and there I saw a *coffin!*

When I went downstairs, Charlie had a cut on her finger and Dracul asked to suck it. We knew there was something suspicious about him.

As soon as we were asleep, Dracul tried to suck my blood so I broke his fangs. I woke the others before he woke up dead spirits. We ran out of the hotel and the funniest part was that Justin was in his *boxer shorts!*

We reported this to the police, so they closed down the hotel and made it into a hall where Justin, Charlie and I taught children about the story of the haunted house and we performed different songs from Justin's album.

Danielle Sherwood (9)
Our Lady Of Lourdes RC Primary School

THE VIKING KING, HAGRID

One day there was a Viking king called Hagrid. He travelled in longboats. He needed about 10 longboats to carry his whole army and he had one particular battle that was bloody and fierce. Even though the Vikings won, about 1,000,000 died. But two and a half million Normans died. They used axes and people threw spears as well.

But the Normans didn't know who was coming. All the Normans saw, were fierce people coming who started looting and killing. The Normans tried to defend themselves, but there were too many Vikings. They imprisoned the Normans and they became slaves.

Michael Gill (7)
Our Lady Of Lourdes RC Primary School

THE DRAGON IN THE PLAYGROUND WHO KIDNAPS CHILDREN

One day there was a boy and girl called Peter and Molly. They were the best friends in the world. They said that if they did not meet each other they would have been sad. Molly always went to Peter's house to stay the night. Peter's mum dropped them off at school. They were bored by themselves. Peter knew it would be hot, so he brought his hat. He took it off to play catch. He asked if Molly wanted to play. She said yes and played with him. They threw it to each other. Peter threw the hat to her but it went into the bush. Molly went to get it and she found a big egg. It was a dragon's egg and it had a baby in it.

The dragon was looking for the egg. He saw Peter and Molly near it so he grabbed Molly and Peter in one hand and with the other hand the egg. The dragon flew up in the sky. Molly dropped out of the dragon's hand. She landed in a bush. She did not hurt herself but she started to smell.

Molly had seen a castle when she dropped out of the dragon's hand. She thought that it might be his house. She went to the castle and took two guns with her. The castle belonged to the dragon and it had Peter locked up in a cage. Molly saw him so she started to talk to him. The dragon saw her talking with him, so the dragon put her in with him.

After a week he fed them beer and bread and water. Peter always had to go to the toilet. Molly gave him a gun and they shot the dragon. He fell straight to the floor because he was dead.

Holly King (8)
Our Lady Of Lourdes RC Primary School

DRAGON ON THE MOON

One day a dragon was in a cave. He wanted to go on the moon but his mum and dad said no. He tried to get out of the cave. When he had got out of the cave he tried to go to the moon again and again, but he couldn't get to the moon.

Then he had an idea. He got a blank piece of wood and a big stone. He tried five times to fling himself up. The fifth time he did it and he was on the moon. He was so happy that he went round and round on the moon. The moon was made from cheese so he was eating the moon, but he didn't eat it all.

He was kind of alone and he wanted to play with another dragon, but no one was there to play with. He wished he had a friend to play with. Suddenly his wish came true. He was surprised and he was so happy. He played with his best friend all day. He played games like Monopoly. That is a good game to play. It is such fun and they played it all day.

`One day the dragon's friend fell off the moon and he never saw his friend again. He was crying a lot. The dragon said, 'Where are you best friend?'

One day he too fell off the moon and he went back to Earth. He went back home and played with his toys.

James Chalk (8)
Our Lady Of Lourdes RC Primary School

DARKNESS

Andrew was walking back home from a dangerously boring day at Kensington High School with his best friend, Charlie, and had just stopped at 'Jim's Corner Shop' for a quick snack. Andrew was a cheerful thirteen-year-old. When he wasn't cheerful, he was serious, but don't let that put you off him. He had dark hair which looked unnaturally greasy, his eyes were a dark acid green, but, there was something about them that you couldn't say was normal. They were different. The day you met him your attention was automatically drawn to them and you thought about what was strange about them. Your mind, no matter how hard you tried, couldn't figure it out.

Andrew opened the door and entered the corner shop; Jim was sitting on the other side of the counter listening to Radio 4 as usual. Andrew and Charlie had known Jim for three years because they visited his shop practically every day. Jim was a middle-aged man with a small moustache and greying hair.
'What can I do for you today?' asked Jim with a grin on his face.
'I'll have . . . a Snickers and a Pepsi,' Charlie stated.
'And I'll have a Yorkie and a Dr Pepper,' said Andrew.
'A pound each,' Jim said merrily.

Andrew and Charlie continued on their way home, munching their snacks contentedly. Soon they were at the end of Charlie's street.
'Bye, see you tomorrow!' called Andrew.
'Bye!' replied Charlie.
Andrew continued. Charlie lived only a block away from Andrew and met up regularly at the weekends. Soon Andrew was on his doorstep, reading the note on the door. The note read: 'Andrew, your father and I have gone out for dinner, be back at ten, tea in the fridge. Mrs Grimstone will babysit you. Be good, Mam. XXX'

Andrew opened the door, took his coat and shoes off and made his way to the stairs. Mrs Grimstone had already arrived and was sitting in the living room watching a soap on television; she didn't notice him come in.

An electrician was in the kitchen fixing the oven; he smiled at Andrew exposing yellow teeth that, to Andrew, seemed inhumanly pointed. He had seen that face before but he couldn't think where. He went upstairs to his room, dumped his bag on his bed, opened it and took out his homework. He put his homework on his desk, got out his pencil and sat down to work. He was in a daydream when an image flickered across his mind. It was from the TV. Just a year ago there had been a plane crash in Sweden. Thirty-three people were killed, but forty-seven people survived. They were forced to eat the flesh, blood and bones of their crew for three months and thirteen days. There had been pictures of the victims who survived, that was where Andrew had seen the electrician before, that was why the electrician was familiar.

He was just in the middle of a stupid maths problem when Andrew found himself in a sea of pitch-blackness. He looked out of his window and saw that the street lamps were out and the moon and stars only lit his street. Andrew fumbled around in his drawers looking for his torch. When he eventually found it, he heard voices downstairs.
'No, no don't, please,' shrieked one of the voices.
'Why shouldn't I?' hissed the other one.
'No, no, please, *argh!*' screamed the first one.

Andrew descended the stairs carefully, avoiding any sound that would give his position away. He crept silently to the door of the living room and listened. He heard a ripping sound like someone ripping a tablecloth in two. Then he did the most stupid thing he could have done at the time; he leapt into the room shouting, 'What are you doing?'
The second he landed in his living room, he froze on the spot shaking, his mouth open. Right in front of him was a man holding a severed arm, like a huge chicken leg inches from his mouth. All around his mouth was blood which was dripping onto the blue carpet which was now red with blood. On the floor lay a bloody carcass of a woman, her neck at a strange angle, bone sticking out of where her left arm should have been, her eyes wide open staring at something behind Andrew. Andrew suddenly realised that the woman on the floor was Mrs Grimstone.

'You!' grunted the man.

Slowly he advanced on Andrew. Andrew screamed after he swore badly. (Well, wouldn't you if a man you had never seen in your life, a cannibal, approached you in the dark!) Andrew ran to the nearest window, opened it and shouted, 'Help!' at the top of his voice praying that someone would hear him.

At that moment, the man did the strangest thing. He ran out of the door as fast as he could with the carcass, apparently afraid he would be found out.

As soon as the man had left, Andrew shut the front door and ran up the stairs into his room and dived under the covers of his bed. He tried to sleep to avoid being petrified until the morning. Eventually he did.

The next morning, the police and an ambulance were outside Andrew's house questioning Andrew's parents and trying to comfort them. Upstairs in Andrew's room the window was ajar, bloodstains were drying on the bed and floor, the head of Andrew Chanderson lying on the pillow.

Why was the window ajar? How did the bloodstains get on the bed and carpet? Why was Andrew's head on the pillow? I don't know, do you?

Tom Marvin (10)
Oxford Gardens Primary School

SILVERFISH

One night Nona went with her parents to her favourite pizza restaurant. Even though it was her favourite place to eat, she hated the toilets there because she knew they had silverfish skidding across their toilet floor. (Silverfish are nasty little fish that look like commas.) Nona is extremely scared of them.

Unfortunately she needed to go to the toilet after a massive meal.
'Mum, I need to go to the toilet, can you come with me?'
'Nona, you're a big girl now, so you can go by yourself,' answered Nona's mother.

Nona went silently up the stairs to the toilet, tiptoeing over the cracks as if they were splinters. Finally she arrived at the smelly cubicle. She checked for the silverfish, under the seat, in the bowl and behind the pipes, but she couldn't see any. Once she convinced herself that it was safe, she sat there. Secretly a silverfish popped into the toilet bowl without Nona realising.

When she was walking down the rickety staircase, she felt an itch just where her belly button was, but she ignored it. Mum was waiting for Nona at the bottom of the stairs. As they were about to leave, she commented, 'You look pale, are you feeling alright?'
'Yeah, what made you think that?' replied Nona.

As they retreated, Nona's itch moved to the place where her appendix was, this started to worry her, but hours passed and nothing happened (apart from the itching).

That night Nona felt ill and she needed to puke! Nona knelt by the toilet. Suddenly, *burgh,* and sick was spouting out of her mouth. *Silver sick!* Silver sick reminded her of silverfish and she realised they were gushing from her mouth. Luckily it only lasted for one minute! When she finished, Nona rushed to her mum and dad's bedroom.

After the silverfish had been flushed down the toilet, they were racing through the pipes, turning and twisting. Soon the fish were popping up in everybody's water system.

'Mum, I've just been sick,' said Nona queasily.
'Oh Sugar, let's get you cleaned up,' said Mum.
'But it was not any old sick, I actually vomited live silverfish!'
Mum fainted!
'Oh well, I'll take you to the doctor's tomorrow,' said Dad calmly.

The next day, Dad took her to the doctor's for an X-ray and check-up.
'Dear me,' said the doctor, looking at her bony X-ray, 'I've never seen anything like this before!'
It looked like her body had grown extra bones! The doctor examined it once more, a bit more closely.
'It looks like they're fish bones,' said Dad.
The doctor agreed and he was very confused.

Lily, a girl who lived in the same block of flats as Nona, liked to drink straight out of the tap, not in a cup, just straight from the tap. The next morning Lily turned on the tap and gulped down the water continuously. A silverfish trickled slyly down her throat. Lily didn't feel anything.

That day, Lily set off on a holiday to Australia. Lily had a long but enjoyable flight, but, just as she landed, she started to feel ill so she ran straight to the nearest toilet and *burgh,* she vomited. The fish came rushing out of her dainty mouth. Now the fish zigzagged through the Australian piping, they were in a new land!

The human race was slowly mutating into fish-like creatures as they swallowed the contaminated water.

Four months later, the fishy Nona turned on the television and the news was on. The presenter wasn't human, well only half! They were all turning into mutants!

Lavinia Porter (11)
Oxford Gardens Primary School

A Day In The Life Of Eva De Puebla

Hello, my name is Eva De Puebla and I am a lady-in-waiting to Queen Catherine of Aragon. In Spain I used to be like a little sister to her, now she is more like a mother to me. I sit at her feet and help her sew her altar cloth, we talk about things as we do, they are often about things we used to do in Spain.

Usually my sister Maria and I get up early, perhaps five o'clock and help each other to dress, then we go to the Queen and help her. After that it is probably about eight o'clock and we have to go to morning mass. When that is finished, we eat breakfast which lasts around an hour.

Next we go and sit with the Queen in her rooms, they are so jolly. She has musicians play and we take it in turns to dance, everyone is always talking and laughing. Sometimes the King comes in to check on things. He has golden hair with blazing blue eyes; he has a stocky body and plays lots of sport.

Anyway, today was Friday, and we always calm things down on Friday. We woke up at half-past five and dressed, then we had a break of ten minutes before we helped the Queen. After that, we went to morning mass and had breakfast.

It was about half-past nine when we went to watch the King play tennis. He won of course, but his opponent was very, very good. Tennis is always long, but not usually all morning. Anyway, when it was finished, we ate lunch and went back into the Queen's rooms. There was more talk and less work today, for me as well! There was a warm breeze and sunshine so that made us all happy.

Later on we all went for a walk and read outside. We all stayed for ages and, when we got back, it was time for evening mass. When that finished we had to rush and change the Queen and then ourselves.

The King had a beautiful banquet waiting for us, complete with sweetmeats, venison, veal, pheasant and other things such as sugared fruit. Then we all got up and danced. After that I was so tired that I wanted to go straight to bed but I had to help the Queen. When I got to my room, I changed quickly and fell straight to sleep.

Layla Ali (11)
Oxford Gardens Primary School

WHERE ARE YOU?

My name is Maria. This story you are about to read is the most horrible, the most creepy experience I have ever had. Please read this story carefully to get the teeniest, creepiest details.

I went to school on a sunny, winter Wednesday morning. It was five days till we were going on our school journey to the Isle of Wight, and I couldn't wait. It would be so exciting. I felt like I was waiting five years. Anyway, as I was saying, we had a new supply teacher, Mr Spockworth.

'Mr Spockworth is your temporary teacher,' Ms Rayment, our head teacher told us. He walked in after her - a tall man with jet-black hair. He looked about twenty years old. His piercing blue eyes darting around examining each person, as if to take a photo of each one of us to remember in his head. But something happened next that freaked me out; he stopped to stare at my best friend Hannah and me for longer.

I looked at him, so did everyone around me. His pale, white, ghostly skin looked extremely creepy . . .

Well guess what? Mr Spockworth was actually quite normal apart from his appearance and his name, or so he seemed.

We usually questioned our supply teachers about where they came from, but Mr Spockworth remained a mystery.

Before Mr Spockworth and Ms Rayment had come in we hadn't had a teacher, so we had been sitting there waiting. It was about five minutes till break time, so by the time we got started and started to get to know Mr Spockworth, the bell rang.

We all went outside and Hannah and me were talking. The noisy, happy playground was all around us, when suddenly there was a low, loud shout. *'Go to the tunnel!'* It was as if time had frozen. There was a silence. Everyone turned around and looked at the building. The voice, the voice, *the voice!*

The bell rang and sounded the end of play time. It took us about ten seconds to realise it. I turned, shocked, blinded by questions. What was that? Who shouted? Was it who I thought it was? Was I just over reacting?

Just before we went into the classroom we hung our coats up. Mr Spockworth was talking to Hannah and rubbing her head. I hung my coat up and when I looked back Hannah was gone and Mr Spockworth was walking into the classroom. I thought Hannah had gone inside, but I realised, when I sat down, she wasn't there. She usually sat next to me, but her seat was empty. The pages of her open textbook turned as the wind came in through the window as if to say, she's gone.
'Mr Spockworth?' I asked, my hand raised.
'Yes.'
'Um . . . I-I was, er, wondering if you know where Hannah is?' my voice was shaking.
'Oh yes, she had a little headache so she's gone to the office,' he said, then his eyes darted to a small gap in the bottom of the wall, at the back of the classroom; he smiled then looked back at his book.

I waited and waited but Hannah didn't return. I waited through maths and English, but still there was no sign of her. Scared as I was to do so, I asked, 'Mr Spockworth?' I said standing by his chair.
'Yes!' he said.
'Why isn't Hannah back?'
'Well, she's probably gone home.'
'If she had, she would have come up to get her stuff.'

I turned and went to sit in my seat. I was getting suspicious and angry. I kept glancing at Mr Spockworth. Then I had a brilliant idea. I thought carefully. Hannah had mysteriously disappeared, was all I could think of. Once I was looking at Mr Spockworth and he caught me. I quickly looked down and wrote something in my textbook. I wrote:

'Mr Spockworth
'Go to the tunnel'
Hannah and Maria
The small hole at the back of the classroom'

Then he called me . . . 'Maria, please come out of the classroom, I need to talk to you.'

I stood up. Everyone looked up. Their eyes followed us as we walked across the classroom. They all knew this teacher was really creepy and not to be trusted! I knew they would all press their ears against the wall to listen.

Once we were out of earshot, he did something, something weird. What I had seen him do to Hannah, he did to me.

'I am fed up with someone as nosy as you,' he said.

'You've got my friend somewhere,' I shouted as loud as I could.

'Go to the tunnel!'

Mist whirled around me. Everything began to spin. I felt dizzy. I felt sick. Then I couldn't feel a thing. I felt like I was paralysed. I felt my brain was shrinking. Then it all stopped. It took me a while to recover and when I did I looked round. I was in a tunnel and it was dark and dusty. I saw a girl sitting quietly crying, softly.

'Hannah!' I shouted.

She jumped and looked up.

I crawled across to her, as the tunnel was low. We sat there talking about the horrible teacher. I told her everything that I had found out and about the note in my textbook. There were many questions. How would we get out? Why were we here?

***

So here we are sitting, waiting. We have figured out one thing. We are in the little hole at the back of the classroom and we are hoping somebody finds the note I left or that we can think of a good idea for us to get out of here and get revenge on Mr Spockworth. So if you go to Oxford Gardens Primary School and are in 6H-W try and help us to get out. I have sent this story out and I'm hoping someone finds it. I have a few last words. If you find this, please help us. You will be a hero (or heroine) and you would have saved someone's life.

Ameera Rajabali (11)
Oxford Gardens Primary School

LAVA DEATH

Frost drew his cloak tightly around the barren ice caps. Wind and snow worked together as a team howling like a wolf and smothering like a blanket meant to suffocate. Michael Spink and his team struggled through the swirling rage. They were on the most difficult mission in the entire world . . . The quest for the ozone layer. The team's goal was to laser a piece of the ozone layer to take it home so that it could be studied in science labs. Hopefully scientists would be able to create clones, place them in the sea and make it a breathable place.

It was 2.30 in the morning when Mr Spink decided to turn in and set up camp. Little did the team know that their camp lay on the death strip of Mount Saskabab.

Five hours later Michael woke to find more than half of his team dead with frostbite. The survivors were lined up, waiting to have toes and fingers amputated.

Everyone had lost hope, but kept fighting for survival. It seemed to Mr Spink that the ground opened up when his back was turned, because there were less people each time he looked the other way. By the time that Mr Spink had reached the bottom of the highest peak of Mount Saskabab, only Spink and two others survived, but they were at their destination.

The laser was set up, Michael pressed the 'on' button and the whole thing exploded!

Lava is a born killer, it did its job.

Sofia von der Schulenburg (10)
Pembridge Hall School

NIGHTMARE

As soon as Lucy woke up she heard the familiar weekend morning sounds. She jumped out of bed, pulled on her clothes and rushed downstairs. She burst into the kitchen and received the shock of her life. There was no one in there and yet the newspaper had picked itself up and the pages were turning by themselves.

At the stove somebody was putting rashers of bacon on the frying pan but Lucy couldn't see that somebody. At the table the fork laid for her brother was banging on the table, a habit her brother had when he was hungry.

Lucy screamed and ran out of the room. She ran up to her bedroom and slammed the door. She took three deep breaths, then wondered what to do. She opened the door and ran across to her brother's room. She thrust open the door, there was no one there. She tried again with her mother's room with the same unhappy results. Then she remembered the small black phone her mother kept under the bed. Lucy picked it up and dialled 999. She heard the phone being picked up at the other end and breathed a sigh of relief. 'Hello,' she said. There was no answer. She slammed down the phone in frustration. What was happening?

Lucy ran back to her room and cried herself to sleep. She woke up much later feeling refreshed. She ran downstairs where, at the bottom, her brother ambushed her. She laughed and tickled him. He screamed and giggled hysterically.

Emily Strang (11)
Pembridge Hall School

THE MAGIC HORSESHOES

Jock sighed, the flashing bay stallion had come last for the seventh time in the season.

Liberty Freestyle had fantastic racing bloodlines but still he did not have the courage to win. Just as Jock was skidding up the drive in his old Ford horse box, he noticed something glistening out of the corner of his eye. He turned off the humming engine and jumped out, then curiously bent down.

The noise of metal upon metal could be heard for miles around. Fierce sparks of dancing fire whirled up into the dusty sky. The blacksmith carried on working and gradually the vague shape of horseshoes appeared as the metal was moulded more and more.

The stallion's flowing mane blew uncontrollably in the daunting wind. He stood there, sturdy as a rock, admiring his new silver shoes. The early morning dew ran lazily down his perfect hooves as his knowledgeable eyes gazed proudly into those of Jock.

The exciting day finally arrived when Liberty Freestyle was to race in the Scottish Championships. David Baird, the jockey, sat confidently on the stallion's back. The piercing gunshot sounded and the race began. The horses' hearts beat in a rhythm but it was clear that Liberty Freestyle was going to win. He crossed the finish line leaving others behind.

Years later, Majestic Morph, grandson of Liberty Freestyle, passed the finish line first, wearing four shining, magic horseshoes, the ones that had made Liberty Freestyle a champion.

Amabel Scott (10)
Pembridge Hall School

A Tale To Tell

One man decided to go into space to find a different world. He had heard of stories saying there were different worlds, but he wanted to find out if this was true.

He packed up ready for his journey and went off to the station. His spaceship was there waiting for him. He got his suit on, he was ready to go. He got into his seat and he heard the counting down. It said, '3, 2, 1, blast-off!' and the spaceship blasted off.

It had been about a week in the spaceship. He had seen so much. He had seen alien life forms, coloured sky, a desert, a dust storm, meteor storm, craters and other things. The man looked ahead and in the distance he could make out some stars in a circle. As he got closer it had turned into some letters. It now said, 'Future'. The man was amazed at this then it went back into a circle of stars, so he decided to go in the circle.

Inside the circle there was a planet. He decided to land on the planet. As he looked out of his window, he saw people just like him walking in a city. There were huge skyscrapers in the city, lots of cars, millions of buildings and even gas clouds in the sky.

After spending a few days there and writing in his diary, he set off home and became the greatest scientist in the world.

Charlotte Raven (11)
Pembridge Hall School

THE CAT LOVER

When I was young an elderly lady called Queenie lived in our village. She had a beloved cat called Midnight. Midnight won every competition that she entered and always beat the neighbour's cats. Queenie fed homeless cats, even though she had to spend all her money feeding them. Her neighbours were not nearly as agreeable as Queenie.

The neighbours were so annoyed that their cat always lost to Midnight, that one day they asked Queenie if they could borrow her. Queenie, of course, let them have Midnight. The neighbours entered Midnight in lots of competitions but she always lost. The neighbours grew so cross that they hit Midnight on the head with a spade. They returned Midnight saying there had been an accident.

A year later, there was a drought. Nobody had any food, least of all Queenie. Queenie soon ran out of food to feed her cats with, so she went to Midnight's grave and prayed for there to be enough food for all the cats. Later, when she emptied the food bowls, she found they filled up again.

The neighbours, seeing this, went and stole the bowls while Queenie's neighbours didn't join in. You see, though the drought had ended for the rest of the village, it hadn't ended for Queenie's neighbours. I still see them today, begging for food.

Molly Powell (11)
Pembridge Hall School

The Tinker's Tale

Emma and Isabella Stuart lived in a remote glen in the Scottish Highlands and every so often an unusual character would enter into their midst.

Jock McTarmac was a tinker who came from time to time to play the bagpipes and tell the girls and their mother fairy tales. He used to tell the girls that he had been in the army with their grandfather, but they knew this was not true as their grandfather had been in the navy.

Mrs Stuart used to give Jock scones, but she always joked he would have preferred a glass of the golden liquid, and a few pounds for his troubles.

One cold autumn day Mrs Stuart and the girls went for a stroll in the glen. Then it struck them that Jock hadn't been to see them for two weeks. *Oh well*, they thought, *he has probably moved.* Then suddenly their eyes met with part of a body at the foot of a large oak tree. They moved closer, the fear mounting up inside them, then the reality struck them as they saw a patch of tartan cloak and smelt a whiff of familiar whiskey . . . it was the lifeless Jock.

Emma and Isabella wept and Mrs Stuart was close to tears as she comforted them. They didn't understand why Jock had died, she suspected it was from drinking too much whiskey.

Sadly she rang the police and an hour later his body was driven off.

Part of their childhood had died with Jock that day.

Anastasia Pejacsevich (11)
Pembridge Hall School

JOCKEYS

Anna was a 12-year-old girl who lived with her mother and father in Surrey. She had mud-brown hair and olive-green eyes. Anna was good at lots of subjects, but her favourite thing to do was ride. She was the best rider for miles around and for her 12th birthday she was given a beautiful jet-black horse she named Midnight.

One morning in early spring, Anna received a letter from her riding stables where she kept Midnight. She rapidly opened it and felt a thrill of excitement rush right through her. The National Horse Riding Championships were coming up and Anna had been nominated to ride for the town.

A week later, when the forms had been signed and delivered, Anna set to work. If she wanted to win this trophy she had to work extremely hard. The riding stables provided an instructor and after school every day, she went to the equestrian centre where her instructor and Midnight were waiting.

The Championship season came and Anna was shaking with excitement. The day before the contest she went to the arena and the cross-country field to have a quick run through before the big day. The cross-country was going well until Midnight slipped on the water jump and Anna fell off. The water gave her a softer landing but it didn't prevent her from breaking her arm.

Anna couldn't take part in the Championships, but she had plenty of time for next year.

Isabella Olex (10)
Pembridge Hall School

My First Bullfight

The doors clanged behind me as I walked into the ring. The doors on the other side of the ring were opening and out came a bull, charging towards me. My mind went blank and I completely forgot what my teacher had taught me. I'd never fought a bull this large before or with a crowd of a thousand people. My heart was thumping madly. When the bull was only a few metres away my mind switched back on. I swung my red cape to the side of me and the bull ran straight to it. I whipped it up just before the bull hit it. The bull ran on and then turned to face me again; I jumped round to face it and flung the cape out.

I repeated this again and again until the crowd started chanting, 'Kill, kill, kill the bull.' I looked at the crowd who were jumping up and down shouting. I then looked around the ring looking for the spear. I saw it on the other side of the ring lying on the ground. I edged my way to it and picked it up and took aim. I flung my arm forward and let go. The spear missed by a few centimetres. I took aim again and hurled the spear into the air. *Hit!* The bull fell to the ground and tried to stagger back up but failed dismally.

Elizabeth Gold (11)
Pembridge Hall School

FEAR

My life is at risk. You may think that witch hunting has since long ended in the 21st century, after reading this you will know how wrong you are. If the witch hunters find me they will torture me and finally kill me, and if they don't their faces will haunt my dreams forever. It is not safe to talk to anyone anymore, as anything I say might bring more people against me.

I hide in the church alone except for the priest, praying that the days may last longer until Sunday because that is the day I most fear. People come in and I have no choice but to hide on the top floor of the church where old statues are kept. I write in this diary and hope someone who will not report this to the hunters will find it. The dread in my stomach is worse than my constant hunger and I do not wish to cry but as I hear them searching for me, every day I can only wait for them to find me.

Last night I crept out of the church and walked a few miles and I can only hope to be away from this wretched place by sun-up. I stared longingly in the window as I passed a baker's shop when I remembered today was my birthday.

These are the last words I will write in this diary and I will not say where I am going so nobody will find me.

Jessica Daly (11)
Pembridge Hall School

A Day In The Life Of My Grandparents

My grandparents - fascinating old things with lots of good and bad memories, half of which they can't remember. I am going to tell you what it is like on an ordinary day at my grandparents - that is as ordinary as one can get with one's grandparents.

'Anne! Anniekins!' Papa yelled. 'It's my turn in the bathroom.'
I opened one bleary eye, and winced as the air hit my eye. 'Papa! Turn the volume down a bit, it's almost five-thirty,' I shrieked.
'Exactly! Your grandmother takes more time in the bathroom than any woman I know. She's way past her time in the bathroom.'
'No, what I mean is, forget it!'
I heaved a pillow on top of my ear.

At nine-fifteen I woke up again. I saw Papa and Granny at the table devouring some vile porridge with cranberry juice sloshed all over it. I sniffed the air. It smelt of . . . porridge.
'There you are Imo, want some porridge? There is plenty left in the pot.'
'No thanks Granny, I think I'll pass on that one.'
'Today we are going to the zoo. We'll see the tortoises that move a little faster than your grandmother. Then we'll go to fancy restaurant. Don't worry, I've glued in my teeth so as they will not fall out like last time!'

My grandparents might come across to you as being plainly weird, but they mean the world to me. I'd be lost without them.

Imogen Parry (11)
Pembridge Hall School

TRUE LOVE

This was the time when people of all kinds feared a monster so ghastly to look at and deadly to touch. It was the age of vampires! However, a dainty creature named Cassandra loved one of these blood-sucking fiends - this was the love of her life. His name was Zorro and he loved this beauty that filled his dreams with great rejoicing of the heart.

The vampires were being killed by people who hated them more than the plague. These people were more venomous than snakes and the kind that went round waving fire on sticks.

The couple's love was stronger than the breaking of day and however loud the people shouted, their love grew stronger.

One glorious moonlit evening the couple met in secret and sat on a bench under a weeping willow and Zorro presented Cassandra with blood-red roses.
'As the petals fall off the shorter I have to live,' whispered Zorro.

Suddenly Cassandra felt a sharp clamping pain on the side of her neck. Her teeth began to grow larger and sharper. She was turning into a blood thief.

The sound of shouting could be heard as a vast crowd surged towards them. A man with flaring orange hair held a stake that could be driven into a vampire's heart. As the couple fled one of the men in the crowd grabbed the hands of the couple and plunged the stake into their hearts as they fell to the ground in each other's arms.

Amelia Brooks (11)
Pembridge Hall School

MAGIC FROM MARY

Mary Simpson was an unpopular girl who lived in a world of bullies. Her apple-cheeked mother perpetually weighed her down with kilograms of criticism, ignorance and treated Mary as if she was a rat. To make matters worse, Mary was bullied at school by a girl called Sally. Many nights Mary cried herself to sleep - was there anyone in the world who loved her?

One grey morning, Mary rose reluctantly from her bed. 'Another day,' she groaned. She was dreading Sally's voice barking in her ears. Mary prevented the tears from streaming down her pale face. She pulled out her Barbie from under her bed and gently stroked its silky locks. Miraculously the Barbie's lips parted and it whispered softly, 'Your wish is my command.'
'I wish I had superpowers,' Mary replied.
Suddenly, the Barbie disappeared. Mary shook herself, what had just happened?

Later at school Mary was eating lunch, when she spotted what she had been dreading all day. Sally and her gang were striding towards her. 'Hello wimp,' Sally jeered, 'have you been a good girl today?'
Mary turned around. 'Leave me alone and stop being a cow.' As soon as Mary said the word 'cow' Sally's human shape changed and she suddenly had the form of a cow! The canteen burst out laughing and Sally charged at Mary, who quickly dodged her and sprinted out of the school, giggling.

After that day the magic soon wore off - so did Sally, who never dared to bully Mary again.

Augusta Bruce (11)
Pembridge Hall School

THE GREAT LOSS

It was the end of August 1944, the warm breeze whistled like a hummingbird. The many fruits on the trees were ripe and ready to eat. The sky was bright blue. You could hear the beautiful birds singing in their bark brown trees.

The Ricklock family had been waiting for some news about their father and husband, Tom. He was fighting in France. No one had heard anything about him for a long while.
'Mum!' shouted Sara, excitedly. 'The post's here.' She ran down the stairs to her mother's side.
Joe came stumbling down. Mrs Ricklock opened the letter and began to read.

As she was reading she dropped down to the sofa under her. Her face went ghostly pale. Trying to fight the tears back she told the two children that their dad had died on the battlefield in France.

Mrs Ricklock slowly read the letter out loud. Even though this was a very upsetting time for them, they were proud of their dear Tom. He was a brave and adventurous man, willing to risk his life for his country.

Two years had passed and the Ricklock family were still getting over this great loss, but the war had ended.

Joe, now nineteen, had started in the navy, knowing his dad would be proud of him.

Summer had come round once again and the family were preparing to go on an emotional journey to France. They were to visit their father's grave and lay flowers on it.

Laura Chautin (11)
Pembridge Hall School

THE COLLECTOR

'Yes, but what is it?'

It was freezing cold on Lyme Regis beach where Dr Darwin was chiselling away, ignoring everything around him. He was getting frostbite and almost dying with numbness, but was nonetheless determined to make the great discovery he knew was waiting for him.

Suddenly his chisel clinked against something hard. His face lit up as he felt a warm surge of excitement running up his spine. Slowly and gently he prised up the rock and gasped at what lay before his eyes. Despite the fact that he was almost half frozen he ran around in a circle five times shouting like he had just won a thirty million pound lottery. He was shakier than a jelly on a roller coaster. He would remember this day for the rest of his life.

He ran to the old red telephone box at the edge of the village to call his professor. With the last pennies in his pocket, he made the call.
'Hello, is that Professor Windermere?' said Dr Darwin, his hand trembling with fear. 'It's Dr Darwin . . . I've found something . . . something so special it could change the way we see the world today . . . it's the first ever found . . . we have been researching it for years.' Dr Darwin was struggling to find the right words in his excitement. 'This will change history forever!'
'Yes, but what is it?' Professor Windermere suddenly cut in, in exasperation.

Oliver Baise (10)
Ravenscourt Park Prep School

THE MONEY LENDER

'Boo hoo!' cried a woman down the end of the alleyway.
Chin Windip, why are you crying? wondered a stranger as he put down his umbrella. The girl had hair making her look like a wild black cat.

'My money! My life! All gone! That coxcomb, Jonny Logog, the money lender,' Chin was saying as she panted like a heavy smoker, 'he said to me that before my father died he borrowed a large sum of money and did not pay it back. Now I have to pay it back or he will steal all my worthy items. I have no money! How will I pay?' she shrieked. She started to pray.
Without speaking, Chong Chang grabbed and hugged her. As he held her in his arms, he thought he knew how to end this.

Later, when they got to Wing Song Square, they found Jonny Logog, the money lender. As they saw him he started to bring out his hand whilst smiling. Chong pulled out his wallet and took out his cash. Jonny got closer and closer. As Chong was just about to give the evil, greedy money lender the money, a pick-pocket snatched the wallet and ran off. Chong and Chin froze in astonishment. They ran. They ran for both of their futures. 'We must catch up!' Ching shouted, as he ran like the wind. The thief was lost. *What will we do?* they both thought, *Our lives are gone.*

Ashley Hunter-Love (10)
Ravenscourt Park Prep School

THE ALIEN

'Joe, breakfast,' called Mum.
'OK.'

It was another day at school. I glanced at my alarm clock. I was late. I ran downstairs and saw a packet of delicious honey flakes, and even more it wasn't open. I broke open the seal and shoved my hand in to find the toy.
'Ouch!' I said.
'What happened Joe?' said Mum in a concerned tone.
'I don't know,' I said in a very puzzled tone.

I poured some cereal. A head popped out. I grabbed it and ran upstairs. I was terrified. Was it hostile? I didn't know. I examined it closely. Suddenly the squeaky brakes of the school bus distracted me. I dashed downstairs.

When I was on the bus I opened my hand a crack and peered in. The sun was in the right place at the right time, so it looked as if it was sparkling. He moved his head and peered back at me.
'Zurg,' it said, like a baby saying 'mummy' for the first time.
'Zurg?' I said, puzzled.
The alien looked at me as if to say, 'that is my word, you can't use it.'
'Hello,' I paused as I tried to make up a name. 'Hello, Orian,' I said.
'Hello,' he said, trying to work out what it meant.
'Wow, this alien talks!' I said. The whole bus turned to look at me.
'Take a look, it's here!' I opened my hands but to my amazement, it was gone.

Nicky Cooke (9)
Ravenscourt Park Prep School

BEWARE

The werewolf lay down ready to pounce on his prey, every muscle in his body tensed like a coil ready to spring. A goat scampered nervously across the deserted graveyard looking for food. It stopped on top of a grave, listening for any sign of danger before eating the grass. The werewolf suddenly ran like the wind. The goat played dead, as still as a statue, motionless. The werewolf was not fooled; he picked up the goat in his fangs and carried it over to the oak tree. The prey was shredded in minutes and left for the flies.

The clock struck one and the werewolf vanished into an old mouldy greenhouse which was boarded up from floor to ceiling.

By morning, the werewolf was beneath the ground, in his lair. As the day progressed the men, women and children of the village became more and more frightened. What should they do? Eventually night fell.

The clock struck midnight and the werewolf clambered up the stone stairway, hoping to catch another helpless victim for supper. He sat up tall like a lamp post.

The people of the village circled the graveyard with burning brands trying to be brave whilst looking for the killer of the animals. The werewolf was unaware of what was happening until too late.

Slowly, silently, the axe head fell. The razor-sharp blade glinted in the moonlight. A bat swooped through the belfry. The villagers returned to their homes. The killer was dead.

Elizabeth-Daisy Knights (10)
Ravenscourt Park Prep School

LIGHT AND DARK

One evening, when I was trying to go to sleep on my straw made bed, I heard my brother, Archie, get up. I decided to follow him into the very dark and noisy jungle. (I was scared of the dark so I took a torch.) I followed until my feet had blisters. He went to the coconut trees where he was really lazy and didn't pick them or climb up the trees to get them. He was really lazy and it wasn't fair on me because I have to climb up them because I'm small.

He kept on looking around in case anyone was watching so I had to blow my candle out in case he saw me. He then climbed up and picked hundreds and put them in a scruffy, old bag and started to walk away, so I had to run back, leap into bed and pretend to be asleep.

The very next morning I told Jasmine and Alex about Archie and how I had seen him in the night picking coconuts.

That evening we all sat in our beds and then, as Archie woke up to go and pick coconuts, we started to follow him out. As he got to the coconut trees we suddenly appeared in front of him. He was shocked and Archie leapt into the air. We asked him kindly if he would go back to bed and not be so lazy in the day.

Issy Pritchard-Smith (10)
Ravenscourt Park Prep School

CREAKY FLOORBOARDS

'Mum, where's my suitcase?' asked Emily.

Emily and her family have just moved into an old manor house but they don't know that the last person who lived there left without explanation.

The manor was a tall, old building, similar to one of those horrible haunted houses you might find in a book or a film. Emily thought it was a creepy, dark house and she did not want to live there.

Emily is a brainy girl who loves horror stories, but she can't imagine what it would be like to meet a ghost in a cellar or attic. Emily is tall and pale with long black hair and big green eyes, very skinny with thin red lips.

'Bye Mum, bye Dad!' said the three siblings.
'Right, let's do some exploring,' said Cathy, Emily's big sister. 'Emily explores the cellar, Tom explores the playroom and I . . . I'll explore the attic.' So they all set off.

Emily walked down the stairs and she caught a glimpse of her younger brother as he also ran downstairs. She walked to the cellar door, stopped, took a deep breath and walked inside.

The cellar was a large, dusty, dark room. She heard a creak and began to shiver and shake. In the background she could hear rats squeal and squeak. Emily was terrified. She made a move towards the door. Where was it? It had disappeared. Emily heard the sound again, but this time with a voice in the background. It said, 'Approach, black death awaits you.'

Alexandra Samaras
Ravenscourt Park Prep School

THE COLLECTOR

'How are we going to get it?' Mbekie paused. He liked the idea of getting half a million pounds from a secret area, but people don't just give you money.

'The men will come and we will dash with the money, simple!'

John seemed to think it was just another day, but it was the day that they would go to a secret rendezvous point and collect half a million pounds from a bunch of chaps they had never even heard of.

It was a boiling hot summer's day and John was waiting in the car for Mbekie to come out of the house. Mbekie came out with a cellphone to his ear in deep conversation. John had absolutely no idea what was going on.

'What was that?' asked John, looking particularly puzzled.

'Oh, nothing, it doesn't matter.' Mbekie waved his hand and rolled his eyes.

The gleaming silver Ford Sierra pulled up in front of the lake, dazzling as the lights of Tivoli. John walked over to the five rather sinister looking men and he was just talking about business, when one of the men drew a gun from a concealed shoulder holster.

'Tell us what you know about your friend, the President Mbekie.'

Suddenly, all of the men jumped on their sides as a car hurtled towards them.

Arthur Parsons
Ravenscourt Park Prep School

SHOOTING

'Have you seen one yet?' Hunter questioned from his slouching position on the dew drenched grass. Derek peered over his field glasses at the ex-army general. On his bushy, bearded face he wore that look of patient suffering that those who knew him had learnt to hate. Derek forced himself to silently count to ten, then slapped on a jovial grin that, in truth, looked like a gorilla suffering from acute indigestion.

'Seem to slip out of view every time,' he said, in a voice suggestive of the noise a piece of metal makes, being crushed. The cause of this sound was Derek straining not to seize his companion's neck and throttle him.

Hunter stroked his gun and yawned, making sure that Derek could see him. He was immensely bored of the outing - mostly because he wasn't allowed to talk. 'Disturbs the birds'. Suddenly, Derek whispered, 'I see one - just there.' With a roar, Hunter raised his gun, fired . . . and missed by five metres. Derek resisted the urge to leap on Hunter and pummell him flat; instead he contented himself with pounding the turf with his muscly fists. Hunter seemed only slightly put out. He took a practise shot at a passing pigeon. The bullet whizzed away in the opposite direction. Derek looked at him. He was just like a pigeon. Hunter had begun to whistle. No, surely he wasn't cooing? Derek gazed at Hunter. Pigeons should be shot, right? Derek fired.

Alex Krook (10)
Ravenscourt Park Prep School

THE FIEND IN THE TAVERN

'By Jove! This is top-notch ale, I could drink this five times a day!'
'Couldn't agree more m'lord,' cackled the evil-smelling barman.

Cockal and Folly Kent were alcoholics. No one could outmatch Cockal when it came to drinking the most. Folly could throw a can five hundred metres if annoyed.
'Eh lord, do you know the blood-spiller, the creature that lurks around this place?' a heavy-eyed drunkard next to Cockal grumbled.
'Oh yeah.'
'Well, I 'eard that the 'Blood Master Tavern', as it had become known, lost five custo'er yesterday.'
'And?'
'Oh just thought you would wanna know,' mumbled the foul-smelling demon.
'Can I get the lords anythin' else?' enquired the barman uncertainly.
'Oh yes, how about some of that booze?' announced Cockal.
'All right, I'll go get some m'lord,' stuttered Cornelius Cheeker.

So the brave warrior stomped down the crumbling stone staircase to be confronted by the usual monster who had bewitched so many, clad in cans and plastic.
'So, back again Cornelius?' cackled an evil voice in the darkness.
'Who's there?' squeaked the terrified popinjay.
'Oh, think I don't know about your little downfall, eh? I think not cad! I won't rest until I see the day you fall. Shall I tell you why? I'll tell you why, you told everyone about me, so I want you to fail in business and rot on the streets, but why do that when I can kill you?'
Death descended from the left and a can from the right . . . '

Folly grinned . . . 'I never miss!'

Jackson Partridge (10)
Ravenscourt Park Prep School

THE CHILD SNATCHER

'Bye Nadine,' shouted Jools.
'Bye.'

Jools ran and then jumped the last three stairs at the front of her school. Jools walked slowly down Derlock Avenue dragging her feet. She thought glumly of her annoying brother at home. Jools tripped and she fell gazing her knee. She turned around and noticed a man dressed in black watching her through beetle-black eyes. Jools kept walking, but slightly faster, she wanted to get away from that man and back home as quickly as she could. She broke into a run, her bag dangling off one shoulder. The man started to run as well. Jools turned down Randle Lane. Seconds later the man skidded round the corner after her. Jools had the disadvantage of carrying her bag, which included all her heavy books, the man dressed in black was about two feet away. His hand stretched out and made a grab for Jools, but grabbed her bag instead. She struggled violently, but it was no use, the man had got a firm grip. Jools screamed loudly. The man made a second grab, this time lucky. He managed to grab her around the waist, lifted her and swung her over his shoulder. He ran on but slower . . .

'She left at about 4.15pm on Tuesday afternoon,' mumbled Nadine whilst sobbing hysterically into her handkerchief.

There was a long yellow police line all around Jools' school. In every newspaper in England it states this is now the third child to go missing . . .

Hannah Curnock Cook (10)
Ravenscourt Park Prep School

THE RUSTLERS

'Huh! Trust us to volunteer for the early shift,' muttered Dick through a mouthful of sandwich, scanning the horizon for 'Silver Fang', the wolf that was attacking local flocks.

'It's freezing', if that's what you mean and I've forgotten my sandwiches,' complained Tom. He was the older of the two and at sixty, was forty-eight years older than Dick. Tom sported a long white mane of hair and two very pointy ears, like a sprite from a fairy tale. He too was looking out for anything unusual.

'I heard that Mr Scarman at Up Sydling Farm had two flocks disappear last week from these attacks.'

'Well that's good for us in one way, his flocks would have put us out of business, forcing us to join up with him, which is the last thing we want to do,' came Tom's reply.

'Have you ever noticed that while one or two of the sheep are chased by Silver Fang the rest of the flock vanish?' said Dick.

Suddenly they noticed two men creeping along the hedgerow, each armed with a pike and staff. At the second man's heel slunk a large silver dog. This must be the dog that had made the attacks.

The first man whistled under his breath to the dog which instantly shot forwards like an arrow from a bow towards a few straying sheep.

'We've got to stop this now,' shouted Dick in his excitement. He pulled a small tin whistle from his jacket pocket and blew a long, shrill blast that shattered the early morning silence. The silver dog immediately changed direction and came running towards Dick and Tom. Tom jumped back a pace in fear. Dick bent his knees and stretched his hand out to the dog. The dog bounded up to him wagging its tail and licked his hand. Dick slipped a collar round its neck.

'I think that our rustling problem is over,' said Dick as he fondled the dog's ear. He looked up just in time to see the two men scramble over the hedge, tearing their clothes on the brambles as they went.

James Armour (10)
Ravenscourt Park Prep School

LOST

From the moment I saw it I knew there was no bigger school in the world. I stood in front of it - my new school. It loomed in front of me like a skyscraper. It was ten floors high and very modern. I stepped inside the large glass doors. I had butterflies in my stomach - or more like snakes. I felt like a little pea about to be eaten.

There were only a few people around. I saw three boys and decided to ask the way to my classroom. I walked over to them and realised they were twice the size of me. I was small for my age, so they were probably about twelve. So I asked them, 'Do you possibly know the way to 3E?' (3E was my classroom.)

One of them pointed a grubby finger towards a flight of stairs that stretched up beyond my sight without my glasses on. I started up the stairs. At the top I saw only one door. It was labelled *Head's Office*. I felt sad. I knew the boys had teased me. I wanted to kick myself. I sat down on the top step and put my head in my hands and silently cried.

The door opened and out came a little girl. 'Are you lost?' she asked.
'Yes,' I whimpered.
'Which class?' she said.
'3E.'
'I'm in the same class,' she said, 'follow me.'
My face lit up. I was saved.

Sam Budgett
Ravenscourt Park Prep School

THE HEARTBREAKER

'India, let's go to my bedroom,' Miranda rasped, 'I've got you something phenomenal!'

They were both very bubbly on their way up the stairs. They noticed a picture of a bright and newly grown lily - and they both secretly felt like one too.

I've got to tell India today, Miranda insisted to herself. *I'll ask her now!* But the poor girl wasn't given a chance to speak; India was off.

'You will not believe this Miranda, I have found my ultimate friend at last!' India reputed. And Miranda *did not* believe it. 'My new bestest friend is . . . is . . . Katherine!'
Now Miranda convulsively let go of her crossed fingers and glared at her *birth mate.* She gulped intensively. How could her birth friend be a best friend with one of her foes? And just how could she have forgotten about someone like her?
'Me and Katherine played together all through break as well as lunch break. I had the best time ever! Do you know what else? She gave me a friendship bracelet and I gave her a Friend's Forever locket, just like the one you are holding. Let's see! Oh my . . . this is the same one!' Miranda spoke with a piercing shrill. *I wonder who she got it for?* she pondered.

'Why does this happen to me?' India cried. 'Why do people break *my heart?* For the first time I was brave enough to ask and I am still unlucky. I only ever ask for a best friend!'

Hiba Saleem (11)
Ravenscourt Park Preparatory School

THE BIG EVENTS

I was so nervous! My heart was pounding and my legs felt like jelly. I swallowed hard. I knew the moment would come soon. Just then it did.

The heart monitor drew a straight line and it sounded an everlasting high-pitched drone that made me feel so alone. The nurses rushed in and I was told to go out. I watched my dad but I didn't cry, knew I wouldn't. He looked so helpless lying there with wires cutting into his skin and his grey hair covering parts of his face. His skin was white which made his lips seem redder than ever in their peace. The nurses brought in another contraption.
'Charge to 300!' shouted one of them. They shocked him, but nothing happened. 'Charge to 500,' he commanded again. This time he made a reaction. The heart monitor made a few beeps and then dropped down again. My own heart took a gigantic leap.
'Quickly, charge 800!'

Just then the heart monitor got back to its usual heart rate. His eyes sprang open.
'I want to see my daughter,' he said quietly.
I walked in and sat on the chair next to him.
'It looks like I'll be staying here for a while,' he croaked.

He was allowed out after a few days and I decided to take him shopping.
'Let's go into Marks & Spencer,' I called as I trotted along behind, carrying all the bags.
'I'll go to the grocers and meet you here in five minutes.'
'OK.'
So we walked away in opposition directions.

A couple of minutes later, I pushed the door open to find a big crowd of peering faces. I fought my way to the front and saw a horrifying sight - it was my dad.

Emily Antoniadi (11)
St Mary Abbots CE Primary School

INTERLUDE AT LUNCH

The table was laid with great care; golden cutlery lined up with meticulous precision, dainty little cups and bowls carefully placed so their complicated patterns glinted and crisp linen serviettes shaped like small yachts stood in each place. The food was fit for kings; exquisite pastries, steaming and frothy cappuccinos and cakes able to make anyone's mouth water. All this for the new vicar; the Raff family were adamant they were going to make a good first impression.

Laura's job was to keep her fiendish little dog, Buster, under control, so whilst her parents had tea with the vicar she played an exhausting game of ball with the beastly creature. Soon, however, she was too fatigued to play anymore, but hope arose when she spotted a toy in the living room. Prudently she opened the door, all in vain. Buster rushed into the kitchen, his natural instinct taking him to food. Laura followed and came face to face with her parents and the vicar. Her parents looked embarrassed as the vicar surveyed Buster with a formidable expression. An exasperated Laura took Buster by the collar to carry him away and drop the dirty ball that was still in his mouth.

The result was . . . unexpected . . . to say the least. As she finally managed to regain possession of the slippery ball against her dog's determined efforts to retain it, it slipped out of her grasp and flew into the air, before hitting the vicar full in the face. He was hit by such a powerful force that he fell out of his chair, but tried to defeat gravity by gripping the table leg with his ivory hands. Unfortunately, gravity won and the vicar fell face down on the lino floor, tipping the table until its entire contents joined him. A delighted Buster rushed towards the food at record speed. The Raffs were horrified and seemed frozen to the spot.

When they finally came to their senses, they sent for the doctor. The vicar turned out to have mild concussion. When he came back to consciousness he immediately uttered a frosty goodbye and fled for the door.

Buster had an overdose of sugar and was ill for a few weeks; this still hasn't put him off cakes though! Needless to say, the Raffs go to a different church for sermons and they will never, never, never invite a vicar to tea again.

Jenny Bates (10)
St Mary Abbots CE Primary School

An Old Umbrella Tells The Story

Hello, my name is Mr U! Stupid isn't it? Well, I don't like it, do you? What do you think about being locked up in a cupboard? Not being used, being thrown about?

OK, I'll tell you my story from the beginning . . .

Right, I was in a sale in Harrod's all by myself when a family came and bought me for £25. I was very pleased that at last someone had bought me.

(And guess where I am now? The Oxfam shop!)

So, they took me back and, as soon as we got home, they put me in the cupboard. I was only used once! When the lady took me out, I broke. Surprise, surprise!

Well, she took me with her anyway, because they didn't have another umbrella. Guess what she did when we got back? She stuffed me in the box to go to Oxfam. Mean, old lady. Trust me, I would have been better off staying in the shop.

Jasmine Coe (10)
St Mary Abbots CE Primary School

A NARROW ESCAPE

It was a lovely morning. The sun was shining brightly and the sky was clear blue. Just as I was going to get some mouldy cheese, I thought someone was watching me.

I looked back but I couldn't stare long, its glistening eyes scared me to death. I ran as fast as I could trying hard not to drop my cheese. Suddenly, I fell on a log. I had broken my leg. It came dashing, and I was waiting for it to gulp me down but it just kept on running. Phew! The cat didn't see me. But then it came back looking for me, the cat's mouth was watering.

I couldn't run well but it was worth it. As I was running past the river, I dropped my cheese.

My foot was hurting but I couldn't stop. I looked back, oh! The cat grabbed me by the paw and ran back, it took about five minutes to take me to its home.

There were four kittens waiting to gulp me down and tear me into pieces. But the cat ate me alone in one gulp. It was a dark tunnel, I slid along the watery slide to its tummy.

My leg was bleeding so much I cried. Suddenly something plopped on my head. It was cat food. By now I was so hungry, I nibbled the cat food.

I tried to get out by digging my tiny paws into the cat's tummy. I had a little swing on the tonsils and as the cat was laughing, I jumped out of its tummy and onto the wet grass. It hadn't seen me, I ran to the place where I belong . . . the bin.

Uyanga Zayamandakh (11)
St Mary Abbots CE Primary School

An Old Umbrella Tells A Story

Hello, I'm Pips and I'm an old umbrella. Now I will tell you my entire story from the beginning until the happy ending.

It was 14th October, 11 o'clock, I was made on Northland Island in an umbrella factory called Raining Time.

After that they put me in a special cover, packed me and put me in a truck. We were taken to Raining Time in Oxford Street, London.

Immediately after I came in the shop a lady called Mrs Piggy and her big, fat dog took me to their house without even paying. When we got to the house they put me in a very dark corner, full of disgusting looking insects.

After three days they got me out of there, but when they saw that my colour of brown had disappeared and in its place there was a very dark yellow and that one of my arms was broken, she took me on the playground of a school called St Mary Abbots.

The children from that school had put me into the bin but then a girl came and took me to an umbrella repairing shop. After I was made like new again, the girl came in and took me to her house and used me every single time it was raining. Even if the story had an awful beginning, it has a happy ending at least.

That was my story! Did you like it?

Ana Maria Indruseschi (11)
St Mary Abbots CE Primary School

A Day In The Life Of Buffy The Vampire Slayer

One day there was a girl called Buffy and she didn't know she was a vampire slayer. When Buffy was walking in the street things were going a tiny bit strange, so Buffy went to visit her friend Jenny.

When Buffy saw Jenny she screamed. Buffy ran up the stairs to Jenny's room then asked what was wrong with her. Jenny said that her mum and dad were missing. There was a note on Jenny's bed saying if they didn't get to the Tower of London by 7.00 then their blood would get sucked to their brain - it was 6.40. Buffy panicked and then realised she had a mission to do. She had to go and save Jenny's mum and dad from . . . Spike, the most dangerous creature in the world.

Buffy set off to the Tower of London where Spike was hanging Jenny's mum and dad from their necks. They were doomed - if only there was a way to get up to the top. Spike accidentally dropped them and they tumbled down and down until Buffy realised she was a vampire slayer and that she could fight those guys. She fought the bad guys and freed Jenny's mum and dad too.

In the distance . . . was Spike and Buffy was ready to fight him. She fought him, then they went home and went to bed. Buffy lay awake in bed thinking what her next adventure would be.

Kerry O'Callaghan (11)
Sacred Heart RC Primary School

A Day In The Life Of Indiana Jones

It didn't seem like acting, what I was doing, it seemed more like real life saving. I didn't win the competition to be scared, but anyway, I did my best. *The music should be coming on,* I thought, *3, 2, 1.*

'Der der der der . . . ' the music went and I swooped down on my rope. *'Cut!'* the director yelled. *'There's no style!'* he continued, damaging my ears - I didn't win the competition for that either. But I stopped listening to what the director was screaming and concentrated on the girl I was supposed to be saving in style.

Suddenly I realised she was surrounded by snakes that weren't computer images and she realised too! My heart was pounding as I tightened my grip on the rough rope.

It felt brilliant as I soared through the air, wind blowing my hair back and nearly blowing my hat off. I lifted the girl up but banged into the scene background which was incredibly painful. I climbed up the rope with the girl in my arms, into the loft above.

There was a loud applause, was that for me? I slid down on my rope and the sound was deafening.
'That was brilliant!' the director yelled even louder than before. 'Can you do it again when the camera is rolling?'

I thought long and hard, this could be my big breakthrough. I could be famous when this movie comes out.

Anna Holloway (10)
Sacred Heart RC Primary School

TOY MADNESS

Kym and Mike were home on their own. They hadn't a clue about anything which was to happen next.

Kym was sixteen and Mike was fourteen. Their parents had gone to a posh dinner party in London.

The phone rang. 'I'll get it,' shouted Kym, skidding on the laminated wooden floor in her thick bed socks. 'Hello!' she announced to the caller.

There was a crackle and someone spoke in a rough, creepy voice. 'I know who you are - ha, ha, ha!' The line went dead. The high-pitched laughter rung in her ears.

'Mike, come here,' Kym called into the sitting room to where Mike was snuggled into the deep leather sofas, scoffing popcorn into his mouth.

'What is it sis?' he asked, his eyes glued to the television.

'It was nothing really, might have been a prank caller. They said that they knew who we were,' Kimberly told her brother.

'Wait a minute Kym, Mum disconnected the phone, so you can't have been talking to this person.'

Kym shivered. 'You know what this means?' Kym whispered. 'They're here.'

At that moment something jumped on Kym's back. It was an army of toys each stabbing Kimberly one by one. Blood squirted from her guts and oozed from her ears and mouth. Mike fled from the flooding army of toy madness.

He scrambled up the stairs. The toys followed him, but Mike was too slow . . .

Emily Durham (11)
Sacred Heart RC Primary School

HOUSE 13

The wind whispered in the sky around the old house. My brain was forcing me through the gate but my heart didn't want to go. My heart was pounding so fast. *Creak! Creak! Creak!* as the gate opened. The front door flicked open like no tomorrow.

'Hello,' I shouted hearing the floor creak like someone was there. It looked like all of the six pictures were watching me everywhere I moved with little beady eyes. The curtain flickered and the floorboards creaked. I thought I was going mad. The hairs were starting to stick up on my neck as I saw a white figure in the shadows. 'I hope it's not a ghost,' I shouted as the figure was getting closer and closer. 'It's a skeleton,' I said. I felt like I was going to die. I was so, so scared. It was unbelievable - I am a teenager now, I should not get scared, but I did - I could not help it as the skeleton was getting closer. Suddenly I could feel myself falling to the floor with his bony hands on me.

He was dragging me into a dark room with just a candle in the corner. I tried to keep my eyes shut but I couldn't. I got up and pushed the skeleton and ran to the door, but it was locked . . . The skeleton came after me and threw me up the stairs. I thought I would not get out of there alive because I was on the floor dying.

'Wake up, it's time to go to school.'

AJ Reilly (10)
Sacred Heart RC Primary School

FOOTSTEPS FROM HISTORY

Lucy walked into her new house. It was late. Lucy's mum and dad were out at a party and Lucy had just come back from the cinema. She flopped down on her bed and fell asleep.

Later, Lucy was woken by the door being opened and footsteps coming up the stairs. She thought it was her mum and dad. She looked at the clock, it was midnight. The door flew open. A man in a green and navy suit stood in the doorway with a gun. Lucy had seen something like him in her history books. He looked like a soldier in World War I. The man's face was as white as snow. Lucy looked around her room for something to protect herself with from the man.
'What are you doing in my house?' the man asked, his pale face frowning. Lucy let out a deafening scream.

An hour later Lucy's parents returned. They saw blood everywhere. A trail of blood started at Lucy's room and lead down to the basement. There they found Lucy lying motionless on the floor.

Months later Lucy's parents moved. They stayed in their new house for almost a year but in all that time they had an unstoppable urge to go back to their old house, so they did.

They bought the house back from a family that were all found dead in the house in the previous month.

One day Lucy's mum went out with her friends while Lucy's dad stayed at home. When her mum got home she found her husband lying pale, motionless and covered in blood on the sofa. On the floor was an army hat!

Isabelle Ferrigan (11)
Sacred Heart RC Primary School

JAMES BOND

'Get him, get him!' they shouted as the sirens screeched behind them. MI6's top agent accelerated through a terrorist command post in his red Ferrari. This was no ordinary sports car, it had an ejector seat, oil slick and heat-seeking missiles.

James Bond was in the centre of an Iraqi desert. He had been sent by MI6 to get information on a highly skilled terrorist and drugs lord, but his cover had been blown when they found his Walther PPK, a true sign of the British Secret Service. Now however, his only concern was getting out, alive.

He was travelling at the Ferrari's top speed, smashing through tents and barriers without any problem until a lorry, fully stocked with oil barrels, exploded and blocked his path. Skidding to a halt on the dusty road 007 quickly made his decisions. In the explosion the lorry had been crushed and made a ramp across the debris. It would be a simple trick apart from one problem. The metal was still smouldering. So James Bond had to be careful that the tyres did not stick as it would slow the car down and he would need full speed to get him through the flames. He could not hesitate, it was his only hope.

He revved the engine, picked up speed and flew up the ramp. He was out, but far from safe . . .

Martyn Campbell (11)
Sacred Heart RC Primary School

A Day In The Life Of Jordan

It was the 13th hour of the 13th day of the 13th month when Jordan asked his mum if he could put new flowers on his friend's grave. AJ's doctors found two strange deep marks and a loss of blood when he died. His mum answered, 'Yes you can, here's £5.'

So Jordan walked round to the corner shop and bought the flowers. When he reached the graveyard, as soon as he placed the flowers on the grave, the sky turned dim. It started to pour down with rain, as Jordan ran for cover he noticed a morgue, but what he didn't realise was that on the door of the morgue it had the numbers 666. The sign of the Devil.

As he shook off the rain and dried his hair, he noticed that there were voices. It sounded like there was a secret meeting going on. Jordan thought, *why would there be a meeting in a morgue?* He decided to check it out. As he crept up behind them he ducked behind a strange wooden box with something in it. Overhearing the meeting, Jordan heard that the Devil was going to send all the demons and vampires to kill every human being on the Earth.

Then suddenly the box opened and AJ came out. He looked like he was hypnotised. Then Jordan realised the two marks on AJs neck were bites and that AJ was a vampire and he was after him. Jordan was trapped and AJ viciously murdered him. 'Arghhhhhhhhhhhhh!'

James Woodhouse (11)
Sacred Heart RC Primary School

HOLIDAY FROM HELL

Lily, Timber and Josh all decided to go to Italy for three weeks of their summer holidays to stay with their Uncle Benedict. They soon found out that their uncle was being blackmailed by the Italian Mafia and decided to find out more. However, something soon went wrong . . .

Woof, woof!

'Be quiet you stupid dog!' shouted the man in the deep, dark purple suit.

'I only wanted to come to Italy for a holiday, but no, we have to get involved with the Italian Mafia,' whined Josh.

'Stop being sarcastic. Timber and I are trying to think of a plan to escape,' Lily said crossly. 'I've got it,' she whispered. 'You know you're good at acting. You pretend to be ill. I will alert the guard and when he opens the door, Timber will bite him and we can run.'

'OK,' said Josh, sounding slightly shocked.

Everything was set.

'Ready?' whispered Lily.

'Ready,' Josh whispered nervously. 'Eugh, ouch, it hurts!' wailed Josh realistically.

Lily shouted for the guard and Timber barked. The man in the purple suit came along and smiled a smile that made Lily's skin crawl.

'I think it was something you fed him, he's very prone to illness, please help him!' Josh's noises were getting louder and it was making the guard nervous.

'Wait a second,' he said in a rough Italian accent.

Lily innocently bent down and whispered, 'Keep it up, I think he's phoning his boss.'

'What should I do Boss?' asked the guard.

'Take him to a doctor under a different name,' commanded a mysterious voice on the phone.

'OK Boss!'

'Right, you three come . . .'

Woof, woof, rippp.

'Aargh!'

'Well done Timber, good job!' said Lily. 'Let's go.'

As soon as they had escaped Lily phoned the police. 'We need help,' she said in her very bad Italian. A riot squad came and sorted out the Mafia mess and as a reward for catching the Mafia gang, the police gave them all a first class ticket back to England.

Kate Lismore (11)
Sacred Heart RC Primary School

A Day In The Life Of Sacred Heart Football Team

Hi, I'm Jordan and I play for Sacred Heart football team. The other members are James Woodhouse, AJ Reilly, Jack Marks, James Ellis, Paul Leahey, Harvey Cook, Joe De Campi and Karl Thornton and we played St Mary's in a very important league game.

At 4 o'clock Sacred Heart came back in the second half after a very poor first half. Sacred Heart were playing against St Mary's who had a 6-2 win behind them.

In the first half, St Mary's put the pressure on and scored a very early-deflected goal. Numerous shots just missing followed this up. Late on in the first half, Karl was on the break, but edged his shot over the crossbar.

In the second half Sacred Heart came bursting out and immediately put the pressure on and were soon rewarded with a goal, scored by James Ellis. We knew we had to win or else we would definitely not win the league.

Soon after, we again received the ball and AJ had a thirty-yard shot that edged over the line. Sacred Heart were on fire and straight away scored a magnificent third goal through James Ellis. There was one minute to go! Sacred Heart were holding on to a 3-1 lead. The final whistle blew; you could feel the joy.

We'd already won one cup and now we were on for the double for the second year running and we knew our chances were great. Well done, Sacred Heart!

Jordan Sandford (11)
Sacred Heart RC Primary School

A Day In The Life Of Westlife

Friday the 13th, 2.30am.

Westlife were still sleeping and they had breakfast in 10 minutes with fans in their hotel.

'Shane, get up now!' moaned Anto their tour manager. 'Nicky, can you get up since everyone else does not want to?'

'No!' Nicky replied in a sleepy mood.

Once the boys were all out of bed and ready they had to go downstairs to the breakfast room and meet their fans.

Finally, half an hour late, Westlife arrived with their fans, but their fans still adored them, even though they had made them wait. They were just pleased they were meeting their idols. All of Westlife were wearing sunglasses because it covered up the bags under their eyes. As they were on tour, they were not allowed to sleep for 72 hours and they were out all night partying in London, so it's beginning to show.

Nicky got call on his mobile. It's Bryan, he's in Ireland with his fiancé Kerry (ex member of Atomic Kitten) who was in labour all day yesterday. She gave birth to a beautiful baby girl called Molly McFadden. She was 8 pounds 12 ounces. Bryan is delighted that he is a father and so he wanted to call up his best friend Nicky to ask him if he would be the godfather of his daughter. Nicky was overwhelmed and said yes to the offer.

'Well the tour is over. It felt like we were running a marathon, but it is over so we are going to party!' Those were the last words of the biggest band since the Beatles!

Kelly-Anne Doran (11)
Sacred Heart RC Primary School

GHOST ON THE RIVER

Twenty years ago, a young girl was walking along a river, searching for the people who had made her a ghost; she wanted to make them ghosts too. She was taken away from her lover for all eternity. She walked and walked to find her lover, but gave up. Then without warning, she disappeared.

'Nick, are you ready?' said Jenny, Nick's younger sister. 'Come on, we're going to be late.'
'Late for what?'
'For the dares at the park. Come on, get dressed.'

It was ten o'clock when Nick was up and ready, but they were supposed to be there at a quarter to ten. Jenny grabbed her brother and ran to the park.
'There you are, what took you so long?' said one of the boys quite annoyed.
'Sorry, my brother took ages to get ready.'
'Well who cares about that, let's play!'
'No,' shouted Nick. 'We need to go to the river to play dares.'
'OK then, let's go!'

They walked through trees, bushes and all sorts of wood-like things. There was something on a bush, then it moved sharply and quickly into another bush.
'Guys, it's a squirrel, look!' said Jenny bravely.
'Erm, Jenny that's not a squirrel!'
'Yes it is!' Jenny turned round and there in front of her eyes was a white shadow, floating over her head. Then it created itself into an image. A young girl floated down.
'Run!' shouted the boys.

They ran, they ran very fast. But Jenny was still there. The ghost came down, its eyes turned red and it said, 'You will pay, you will pay!' The voice got louder and louder. There was a big flash and Jenny fell to the ground. The ghost made a gust of wind and Jenny got blown back and hit her head on a tree which knocked her out. The ghost took Jenny and dragged her into the river. It stopped and with one flash of her red eyes disappeared with Jenny.

Three years passed and on the exact day of Jenny's disappearance someone said they had seen a ghost in a park. Nick looked in the paper at a picture of the ghost and said, 'I know that ghost, it's Jenny!'

That night Nick went to find Jenny on his own and never returned . . .

Tianna Alexander (10)
Sacred Heart RC Primary School

QUEEN ELIZABETH I

'Mum, I'm going out,' called Olivia.

'OK,' said her mum.

Olivia was going out with her friends to give their competition paper back that they'd done. She shut the door and set off with her friends, Katie and Lils (Lily).

'Hi guys.'

'Hi,' they replied.

They set off without a word about the competition, not a word about anything.

While they were on their way they noticed something unusual, something that had never been there before. It was an old-fashioned house. So they dared each other to go inside. But then Katie suggested, 'Pick a number and then add 10.' So they did that and the numbers came up as 23, 15, 12 and 31 and Olivia had to go in the house because she had the highest number.

She didn't complain because she knew the consequences. She went up to the door, it creaked and a mysterious voice said, 'Come in child, come in.' So Olivia went in further and behind the door she saw a middle-aged tall woman. Olivia reached her hand out to this woman, but her hand fell through and back down to her side. She screamed, the others rushed in and the door slammed behind them. They all screamed. Then Lily said, 'I recognise her, she's Queen Elizabeth I.' The others knew this, but their lips were just buttoned together, just like the Queen's cardigan.

Lily ran in a different direction to Katie and Olivia ran the same way.

'Go in here,' said Olivia in a frightened voice.

'I'm scared,' replied Katie.

The television was on. 'Look,' whispered Olivia.

'No time for that, I hear footsteps,' Katie said with a tiny, weenie voice.

'Thank God, it's you Lils, we were frightened.'

Six months later Katie and Olivia were found seriously injured and Lily was found *dead* on the day they went into the house.

Olivia Giacon (11)
Sacred Heart RC Primary School

SCHOOL TRIP

Knock, knock, knock, knock! Ben went to open the door. 'There's no one there.'

'Let me see,' replied Lucy.

There was nothing to be seen apart from the bare landing. On the walls the paint was coming off and wallpaper was peeling.

'I wonder where Miss White is?' Ben said as they closed the door and walked back to their desks. Again they heard knocking, then for a third and fourth time. Ben opened the door and a strange man shot in.

'Hello class,' the man spoke in a deep voice. 'I am going to be your teacher because Miss White is ill.' The strange man walked around the classroom. The children didn't dare speak a word. Finally the man puffed up, 'As you know, it's your school trip, so line up. Chop, chop!' The children stood up and walked into a line a followed the teacher onto the coach. 'It'll take two and a half hours to get to our destination.'

Finally the children arrived outside the hotel. As they walked in the walls were all grubby and as they entered their rooms there were cockroaches all over the shower and in the bath and dirt all over the place. As they went over to the beds they had cigarette holes in the duvet and all dirt over the mattress. The man slammed the door shut and left. A couple of hours later he came back with lots of jelly beans in his hands. The class grabbed them and shoved them in their mouths. After 5 minutes they all fell to the floor.

The teacher who was with them started laughing, but then he could see all their ghost spirits rise up. He was so terrified he jumped out of his skin and fled.

All of a sudden Miss White came crashing in. In the far corner, on the news, on the TV, a man was saying that children had been found dead. Miss White then had a funny thought, *Am I alive?*

Laura Brittain (11)
Sacred Heart RC Primary School

STUCK IN THE MIDDLE OF NOWHERE

I was driving along the dark road when I saw a wrecked house. There were no windows and the roof had half-fallen in. It looked really creepy. I went inside, where to my intense surprise, I saw an old man. He was sleeping on the hard, wooden, dirty floor. One eye open, one eye closed, he got up and said, 'What are you doing in my house?' I screamed and practically jumped out of my skin. *What should I do?* I thought.

I ran out of the wrecked house. It was just rubble, although the old man had called it his home. He was at the half-broken door when he shouted, 'Come back here. I'll get you one day!' I collapsed on the floor. My heart hammering. I hurriedly got up and jumped into my blue, very old car. I put the key in the ignition and started the car. I drove along the rickety, unstable road. The old man seemed to be following me. I drove faster.

The old man was still on my tail. He was like a ghost. His moth-eaten shoes didn't even skim the rough tarmac road. He was yelling, 'I'll get you one day!' At the top of his croaky, ghostly voice. I sharply turned a corner. I thought it would shake him off. How wrong was I . . . ?

Kate Bracken (11)
Sacred Heart RC Primary School

UNLOVING FAMILY

'Alicia darling, come in out the rain. Claudia take everything in from the car and then unpack it.'
I sighed as I realised I wouldn't get to finish my book or study. I looked at the castle we were moving into; it was old and very scary.

Later on that night I heard a slow moan as I was reading. It was midnight. I crept down the stairs to the cellar and there, standing in front of me, was a ghost! Before I could run away the ghost had magically locked the door.
'Right you are, a Yank are you not?'
'Yes, what do you want?'
'I want to tell you the story of my life. I was a young woodcutter, living in this house. The very first time I met the owner's daughter I fell in love with her and she fell in love with me. We were going to run away with each other, yet her father brutally murdered me in this home. Then, we were reunited as she killed herself. Now we wish to have a daughter, you!'
'Me?'
'You!'

The woman came out, I was taken aback, the woman looked beautiful. At that point I wanted to be their daughter.
'Do you have books and schools in ghost land?'
'Yes, so will you?'
I thought that I had no life here. My family wouldn't miss me. So after a scream and a bang, I became a beautiful ghost.

Eleanor Rooney (11)
Sacred Heart RC Primary School

THE LAST ONE LEFT

It was 17th May 2003. Stepping out of the corner shop, my hands grasped hold of bags of sweets, which I couldn't wait to devour.

Everything seemed normal until I noticed the silence. No normal sounds, just peaceful tranquillity. Except tranquillity was supposed to be relaxing, but this was just too quiet!

I looked around, scooping my knotty ringlets behind my ears. There, right in front of me, was a trail of dust which, when I followed it, led my eyes through a row of abandoned cars, streets of emptiness and stillness throughout the town. It was like the world had stepped into some kind of motionless silence. My heart started to pound, racing against the clock.

I dropped the bag, not caring that my entire life savings of £5.94 was spent on the contents inside them. I ran towards my house. Beads of sweat trickled down my forehead. I charged into the tall, red brick building, which I called home. No one was there. I ran out of my empty house and I stepped inside a phone box. I picked up the receiver and I was about to dial the emergency services when I realised the phone was dead. I tried my mobile. All I heard was an annoying voice saying, 'I'm afraid your call has failed.'

'Mum, Mum, where are you? Anyone? What's happened?' I cried, petrified.

Then it came to me, I must have been the last one left.

Maya Alvarado (11)
Sacred Heart RC Primary School

THE HAUNTED HOUSE

One night in November, the moon was full and the twins named Louise and Thomas needed some adventure in their lives. So they put on their winter boots and set off into the night, after dark.

While they were walking, they noticed something very suspicious about a house that they had never seen before. It was a few roads away from their own house. All the windows were broken and smashed, the door was wide open and that nowadays is quite odd!
'Let's go and investigate,' shouted Thomas at the top of his voice.

So they went in, not knowing what to expect. As they walked through the door they saw a picture of two people around the age of thirteen, (their own age). 'I wonder whose house this is?' stuttered Louise. 'I wouldn't like to live here!'
'Neither would I! I would hate it!' Thomas suggested.

The twins walked on through the house slowly and quietly. At the top of the staircase they saw a door moving from side to side. They stepped forward and peered through the door and there, right in front of their eyes, was a *ghost!*

The ghost had a chopped-off head which was only hanging on by a thread. It was gruesome!
'Aarrgghh, a ghost!' they screamed. Then the ghost faded.
Was it only their imagination?

Emily Morris (10)
Sacred Heart RC Primary School

THE LOST GERBIL

'Mum, can I have a pet gerbil?' I asked.

'Yes, we will get it right away,' my mum responded.

Once we had come back and put my gerbil in the cage, we all had a little peep at my beautiful, fuzzy, black and white gerbil called Pebble.

'Bedtime,' screeched Mum from upstairs.

The next morning we had some tasty breakfast and as we were feeding Pebble I realised that he had gone. 'Mum, Pebble's escaped,' I said in a panicky voice. We were looking everywhere for her, even in the bin and things like that, on the roads and on top of cars, but we still couldn't find her.

We looked at the last road near my house, we panicked but there was some sort of blob on the road, lying as still as a statue. 'Pebble, she's here Mum,' I screamed as loud as I could. I ran hurriedly feeling suspicious, wondering how she had escaped. When we saw her we thought she was dead, so we took her to the vet's and the vet did something, I don't know what, but that doesn't matter.

'She's alive,' the vet said proudly.

'Yeah!' I yelled.

So Pebble was alive and we were happy for the rest of our lives.

Samantha Anthony (8)
The Falcons School For Girls

MY SHELL

Inside my shell it's smooth with the odd bump and ripples of shimmering silver that sparkles with millions of rubies on the edge. In the middle are another two million gems of all different kinds, silver, gold, green, blue and bronze. My shell has caves of all different kinds of jewels. In some caves are gold, but all are magical. There is a mirror or magic that comes out of it. An old ship covered with coral in the sea that now has gone. The edges are ragged with sharp knife blades.

On top of my shell are volcanoes that have just erupted with colours of red, white and a pinky-reddy colour. Inside the volcanoes are sparkling pieces of ash. Some volcanoes are closed up like a scab or a wound with tiny, black spots with hairs around. In the middle, wrinkles white, red, pink with the old black mole. White patches with more brown spots on. On the other side is a swirl with glittering stones of gold, purple, silver and blue just like a snail's shell, but a lot more still.

My shell has now got washed up on the sandy, pebbly shore to be smashed and thrown against the stones. My shell might be looked after by someone like me or just left.

Natasha Doyle (8)
The Falcons School For Girls

An Experience To Remember

Another boring Sunday. Mum's off to bingo and I've been dropped off to some place to share a life with an old, boring person. He must be about seventy and I'm there for three hours.

'Why can't I play basket ball (I'm crazy about it) or roam around?' I said sadly.

'Come on, you're going to be late,' said my mum.

I went and slammed the door behind me. I walked to the bus stop in the rain.

When I reached it I stood in front of the cottage. It was quite like the Victorian ones. I went in, there was someone sitting in a rocking chair. The man had grey, scruffy hair. He turned around and gave me a shock. He had black teeth and wrinkles on his face. He was wearing a ragged jacket with torn jeans.

'Hello, sit!' he roared.

I sat on the stool and he stared at me.

'What is it?' he said.

To be honest I thought he was lost in his own world.

I asked questions about his life, like what his ambitions were? I thought he wasn't going to answer, but to my delight he said he was a basketball player. I got so interested that I wanted to ask so many questions about how to play properly and how it felt to be a professional.

Three hours flew by and my discussion was nowhere near finished. I discovered old people aren't so boring and to be honest, it was the best experience of my life.

Saanya Sharma (10)
The Falcons School For Girls

THE HAUNTED HOUSE

Sarah clumsily walked along the old, cobbled street. It was a cold Wednesday morning, she had been in so much trouble in school earlier and decided to leave during the break. She stared into space; not knowing what to do or where to go. She couldn't go home, her mum would go ballistic and no way could she go back to school.

Sarah came to a strange, tall, grey building. She realised the shiny, oak door on it was wide open. She peered inside. There was nothing there, just old, ugly, grey walls. 'Surely there would be nothing wrong with just taking a look?'
She stepped inside and felt a cold shiver going down her spine. She heard a faint whistling noise coming from upstairs. She slowly crept up the creaky steps.

Peering through a door on the landing, she saw duvets, wardrobes and all sorts of strange things flying about in the room. She quickly ran down the stairs, stumbling and tripping. She ran to the door, but before she could reach it, it quickly slammed shut. She could now hear footsteps coming down the stairs.

There was only one thing she could do. So she pulled off her shoe and threw it through the window. She quickly climbed out, leaving her legs bleeding from the glass. What on earth was she going to say to everyone back home?

Emily Neill (11)
The Falcons School For Girls

THE SEASIDE GIRL

Daisy sat on the shore on Rocky Beach. The waves whacked against the rocks which broke them down like fairy powder. Her fair brown hair blew gently with the wind. The dolphins leaping in the sea reminded her of a lullaby her father had taught her when she was only five.

Daisy looked out far beyond the sea. Tears trickled down her soft, peach face. Soft heartedly she hummed the tune. Memories overwhelmed her. Clouds loomed over her. Rain thundered. She got up and wrapped her coat around her and ran to the nearest shelter. Unluckily it was a cave. She had been told too many stories of how people had died in caves, but never what to do if you were in that situation.

Crack! The thunder scared her. She had no choice. She hid in the cave. Walking in further and further, she found something quite unexpected. She found a little girl sitting on some rocks. Daisy and the girl talked about themselves for about half an hour, but for some reason the girl didn't say much about her life. Once the storm had stopped, the girl glided out, turned her head and gave a little giggle. Jealousy crept on Daisy. She had been trying to glide for years now. The girl crept up behind Daisy and reached for her neck . . .
Screech! 'Oh no! Mmuumm the video's broke!'
'Argh!'

Kiran Dulay (10)
The Falcons School For Girls

THE DESERTED HOUSE

'Please Jenny,' Caroline said desperately. 'Please come with me.'
Jenny shook her head, disappointed. 'You know I can't, Caroline. I've got more important things to do.'
'Please,' Caroline begged her. 'You know I like adventures. Don't be so weak. Come on, do it!'
Jenny looked up and a fake smile spread across her face. 'OK, I'll do it on one condition.'
'Anything,' Caroline pleaded, almost kneeling on the ground.
'You do my homework for me at lunch because it needs to be in by the afternoon.'
Caroline sighed. 'OK.'

It was dark and smelt damp. It definitely suited being called a haunted house. Caroline knew it seemed ridiculous, but it hadn't been seen for at least a hundred years. Caroline jumped as she heard a noise behind her. Jenny laughed, 'Only me,' she said.

Caroline and Jenny tiptoed onwards into a dark and dismal kitchen filled with cobwebs with big black spiders hanging from them. It led into a living room with sofas with all their foam coming out. It gave Caroline the creeps.

Caroline peered around the first room upstairs and turned to tell Jenny, but she noticed she was gone. Her brow started sweating and she lifted her hand, wiping it. 'Jenny,' she whispered frantically, 'where are you?' She had to find her.
Although it was pitch-black, she found her way to the stairs. Just thinking about that room made her shudder, the perfectly made bed. Suddenly she bumped into someone. It was Jenny. 'Ha, ha, I made you scared,' she laughed.
Caroline, now quite annoyed, beckoned her into the living room. Suddenly there was a flash of light and Caroline and Jenny vanished for good.

Sanjana Kapila (11)
The Falcons School For Girls

MISS FOXLEY

'Hello, and welcome to the Ritz Hotel,' said the receptionist politely.
'George, will we be staying here forever?' asked Sophie.
'No, of course not, just until things have settled down at home!'

'Yes, I was booked in for . . .' Sophie sat on the blue, bouncy chair, thinking about what happened last night. She stared at the gold-rimmed, glass, rotating doors, watching every person come in, analysing their personality from what they were wearing, their face shape and hairstyle.

Sophie turned round and looked at her big brother who was smiling and acting 'cool'. He wore his black leather jacket, dark sunglasses and chewed his gum with his mouth slightly open. Sophie continued to watch the people coming in.

Suddenly, through all the dull, dark colours, she saw a tall, skinny lady with dark hair as pitch-black as the midnight sky, up in a bun, with lips red as a rose and a long, blood-dripping red dress with black leather shoes. Long, pointy fingernails stuck out of her long, pointy hands. The cape she was wearing was of tiger-skin and as it happened, Sophie's favourite animal was a tiger so she got annoyed, very annoyed. Hung around her neck was jewellery, not diamonds or rubies, but teeth of tiny cubs, but Sophie was horrifed by two rather long, white ivory tusks. In the lady's hand was a poor crocodile handbag, brown and scaly. Sophie was not happy at all.

Beside her was a girl of Sophie's age, a spitting image of the lady . . . a sort of mini me, Sophie guessed, except with short, ginger hair.

Sophie was mad, really mad . . .

Olivia Lo (10)
The Falcons School For Girls

TIDY UP YOUR MESS!

'I won't tidy up your mess. I won't, won't, won't!'
I ran out of the house, slamming the front door. I walked along the grey gravel and down the road without looking back. Why should I tidy up their mess? Suddenly, I tripped over an old brown book with gold letters saying, 'Hercules' Diary'. I knew I would have to report it to the police, but I decided to look inside. Suddenly, there were colours flying around.

'Ouch!' I had landed on sandy ground. *I must have landed in a school play,* I thought to myself. At that moment, a chariot came by and a load of sand blew in my face. I then realised I wasn't in a school play, but I had gone back in time to the Greek period.

Turning around, I saw a guard. Quickly I ran and tried to hide behind a barrel of water. But it was too late, the guard grabbed my arm and took me into a great palace and went into a huge room.
'What do we have here?' bellowed the king. 'Where do you come from?' he bellowed again. 'Ah ha.'
There was a huge bang and a muscly man came in.
'Hercules has killed his family,' announced a guard.
'You will clean out King Augustus' stables and take this girl with you.'
Hercules grabbed me and flung me over his shoulder and set off.

When we arrived, I stared in horror and screamed out, 'I won't tidy up this mess. I won't, won't, won't!'

Zofia Jonas (10)
The Falcons School For Girls

THE SHELL

The shell is so smooth, probably as smooth as the silky green seaweed that has brushed past it under that aquarium of fish. The shell is the shape of a horseshoe and it's a chestnut-brown.

On the front there are small volcanoes that are waiting to erupt, but they will have to wait for a few years before they can erupt and leave a dark peach colour. In-between the volcanoes is a lipstick-pink, with microscopic white dots, like snow. On the front, it is rough and hard.

Thea Hemming-Brown (8)
The Falcons School For Girls

THE KUNG FUNG GERBIL

The Kung Fung Gerbil wears black clothes and carries a spear that is brown and green. He carries this everywhere. His face is small, pointed, and he has red eyes and fur that's black-brown. He has big, long teeth. If you touch his back, he jumps out and fights with you, so you have to be careful. The Kung Fung Gerbil eats veg, fruit, seeds and dried fruit, and he drinks water.

He always fights other gerbils, but they are all to scared to fight back. Once, when a Ninja Gerbil hit him, he hit the Ninja Gerbil even harder.

Once, he was fighter of the year, because he survived after fighting 100 Ninja Gerbils. He said in gerbil language, 'It's because I have sharp claws and I've had practise.'

Sharnie Hobbs (9)
The Falcons School For Girls

ALL ABOUT HAMSTERS

Hamsters are nocturnal animals, which means they sleep during the day and wake up during the night.

Hamsters have special pouches in their cheeks in which they can store food. This is a very good strategy because in the desert, where they originated from, they have hunting enemies. They have these special pouches because in the desert, they have to go out to get something to eat, so they scuttle out of their burrows and find something to eat, and when they've found the food they want, they store it in their cheeks and hurry back home. This way, they're less likely to get caught by their predators. They also use this strategy to store food for the winter.

So please bear in mind that if you get a hamster and it's a dwarf Russian hamster, it doesn't like to be kept alone, so you should get a companion for it, then it'll be happy. But make sure they aren't boy and girl! Otherwise they'll mate and have lots of babies!

Katerina Goussous (9)
The Falcons School For Girls

THE BAD WITCH

From the little wooden cottage on the top of Witch Land, the bad witch was cooking up a spell to make all the human people die, so she could rule the world. The bad witch commanded all the witches to gather round her house. She chose three witches to come and finish the spell.

After the spell was ready, they all set off on their brooms. It took three days to get there. When the people saw the witches, they tied to hide. They showered the city with their potion and it landed on all the screaming people, but the people didn't die!
'I wonder why they are not dying?' screeched one of them.
Suddenly, the witches looked down and saw a monster. It was green with yellow and red dots.
'Where did that come from?' shouted Wilma.

They rode back and made another potion, *How To Make A Monster Die.* After they had made the potion, they made their way. When they got there, they poured the mixture on the monsters and watched joyfully as they drank it and died. The monsters ate it because they liked the smell and taste. Then the four went back home and never had to bother with that town again.

Evie Griffin (8)
The Falcons School For Girls

Wow!

It was Saturday afternoon and there was a girl called Ally. It was her birthday and she was very excited. She couldn't wait until she opened her presents. The first one she opened was from her brother, it was a beauty set that she had always wanted. She jumped up and down and started to hug him. The next one was from her parents and it was in a box with padding all around. She took it out and observed it, she realised it was a china doll.

It had hair that was as brown as a coconut shell. Her cheeks were the colour of peaches, her lips were the colour of cherries. Her face was pale white, like snow, and she had sky-blue eyes. She wore a crimson-coloured dress with maroon dots. Her shoes were a sandy-yellow colour and she was also wearing shocking pink socks. Ally loved her, she called her Lissie doll.

Ally had had a great birthday and couldn't wait until she had her next birthday. Lissie doll and Ally never stopped playing all day long.

Hope Hurst (9)
The Falcons School For Girls

GOLDIE THE GERBIL

'Look at Goldie. He's trying to get out!' exclaimed Natasha.
'He won't,' called Samantha.

Goldie is a male gerbil. He is a school gerbil and has shining golden coat with shimmering red eyes. His whiskers are clear as crystal.

In the afternoon, Samantha and Natasha are going to look after Goldie. They were giving Goldie crunchy carrots, fresh lettuce, tasty peanuts and hard sunflower seeds. Just then, Goldie jumped out of the cage and leaped out of the window.
'Oh no!' Mrs Tomlinson, their teacher, shouted.

Meanwhile, Goldie was admiring the large school building. Suddenly, a pitch-black stray cat with messy fur grabbed Goldie by his tiny body. The stray cat zoomed into a pile of dirty rubbish. The cat sat down to have its delicious meal. The hungry cat's mouth was just about to gobble Goldie with one gulp, when someone snatched Goldie out from the cat's paws. It was Mrs Tomlinson.

When Goldie got back to school safely, everyone in the class cried, 'Goldie, don't run away again!'

Emi Iida (9)
The Falcons School For Girls

THE FEATHER

Long and smooth, with golden feathers, it used to fly, but it's beauty is gone. It's ever so fragile, I can't stop thinking about her. The scratches are hateful, but I have to face them.

The sounds of the air that makes my love drift away. The tickles, it makes me laugh away. But the bone of my loved one has gone away. It's rusty and old and bony. I don't ever want to see my plume again. But my love feather, so innocent and lonely, so beautiful and fair, she is my prized possession.

Sanam Kumar (9)
The Falcons School For Girls

My Old Grandma

My grandmother is the most mysterious, melancholic, callous, malicious grandmother in the whole universe. She is not a nice, ordinary grandma, who smells sweet, acts sweet and loves her little children. My grandma doesn't care about me! I live with her you see and the thing I dread most is tea. It's a sort of white, chunky mixture which makes you take 30 million calories just by the look of it. I used to like her, enjoying pulling her false teeth which were covered with the last centuries' meals. My grandmother is wrinkled as an old handkerchief, and as boring as one too.

Anyway, when I was five, my parents died on a plane while I was with my gran. It was then that my life was turned into a blur. I couldn't stand it. She was really mean to me, so that's when I fixed up a bubbling plan. I gently took the white spirit she splashes on her baggy dress every day (she wears a horrible necklace which reminds me of hare droppings.) Taking the product, carefully I poured it into a huge pan, then I went up to Gran's bedroom and took her stinking, steel chamber pot which was full of urine, and dumped it into the pan.

My gleaming eyes searched the tumble-down cottage and I saw her sleeping on a rough chair, snoring like a grandfather. Cautiously, I took my grandpa's rod and started fishing for her false teeth. After a long search, I found them. I dipped them into the urine and boiled them. It had a terrible pong, which I can still smell today. Then I heard this hoarse voice, 'David, is my dinner ready?'
I responded brightly, 'Yes, Gran.'

When she tried it, the liquid attacked her, making her boil, sizzle and steam. Maggots started crawling out from her hairy nostrils. Then she shot up through the roof, like a gleaming rocket, and that was the end of her!

Coralie Malissard (10)
The Falcons School For Girls

HAUNTED HOUSE

After school, me and some of my classmates had a game of cricket in the park. When I arrived, I picked up a bat. Kirsty grinned at me in a spiteful way.

'Oh look who's here,' she sniggered, 'it's Miss Hannah, who's always boasting of how good she is at cricket.'

I ignored her and as she bowled the ball to me, I slammed my bat at it and the ball shot over the fence and crashed through a house window.

'Oh, now you've done it! that was the only ball we had,' snarled Kirsty, frowning.

We stared in shock at the house it had gone it. It was the old, shabby house, once owned by an elderly lady who had died in it.

'Well, you go get it,' said Helen.

'I dare you too,' whispered Kirsty, 'or are you scared?'

'Of course I'm not,' I said, shaking.

As I walked up the path to the door, I saw for a second, a pale white face staring down at me from one of the windows. I gasped and shook my head; the house was deserted, everyone knew that. As I clasped the doorknob, it swung open. I stepped onto the creaky floorboard and jumped as the door swung shut behind me.

I looked everywhere. It seemed pairs of eyes were looking at me. Dust sprang up as I walked, my spine had a prickly feeling. I pushed cobwebs out of my way as I crept up the staircase. In one of the rooms, a sleek black cat brushed itself around my legs. I wondered if it was a witch's cat. My heart thumped, my hands shook as I drew the curtains so I could see in the dim room.

Finally, I saw the ball, but I also noticed a tall figure with curly white hair and an old violet dress grinning at me, showing her crooked teeth.

Shannon Hayes (10)
The Falcons School For Girls